Pick of the Litter
A Holiday Pet Sleuth Mystery

M. Culler

Copyright Information

Contact Information:

https://ghostsintheink.wixsite.com/mculler

mcullerauthor@gmail.com

This is a work of fiction. Any resemblance to individuals, either real or fictional, is strictly coincidental and not intended to depict or offend anyone.

The author holds all rights to this work. It may not be reproduced or distributed in any form, mechanical or electronic, without the author's express permission and consent.

Cover Art: All images are free for use and in the public domain. Cover Design by V. McKevitt.

Table of Contents

Dedications

To Phil, Morgana, and Malcolm- You love me, cheer me on, and put up with me. I love you so much.

To my parents, who encourage me, from scribbles to publication.

To Grandma Gladys. I know you're smiling. I wish I could see it.

To Tabby, Twinkle, Rosamunde, Ein, Brahms, and Rascal- the cats and dogs who leave pawprints on my heart.

To Annee Jones, who organized this whole shebang.

To the students who come to Mrs. Culler's Writing Club. You make writing cool.

To Judy, my darling editor.

To Rachelle, Jen, Laura, Sara, Shannon, Evan, Hebi, Kathleen, Katherine, Steve, Kathryn, Lauriel, Terry, Sofia, Michelle, Dawn, and Lolo—you talk me off of ledges that I build all by myself.

To The Mid-Atlantic Authors' Society and David Stockar, my partner in crime.

To Harry, the memoirist, book maven, one-man PR firm, and mobile therapist. You are valued and loved.

Soli Deo Gloria.

Introduction

A litter of puppies. A mysterious craftsman with a beautiful secret. A stubborn, spunky terrier. Can Fiona solve a Mother's Day mystery?

Spring means it's time to bloom, but Fiona Milton is stuck in "blah." Her love life has stalled, her dreams are on hold, and even Macbeth, her faithful terrier, can't tug her out of this rut.

But a litter of puppies left in her yard might just do the trick! The hunt to find their rightful owner soon has Fiona helping a handsome stranger with a precious secret he needs help to protect. Could Fiona's life be back on track—or will disaster rip it away just as she opens her heart?

Join Fiona and Macbeth as they solve a mystery that will lead to adventure, romance, and a new chance at finding a fur-ever family.

Pick of the Litter by M. Culler is a cozy mystery with a twist of holiday romance that you're sure to love! Check out the other books in the Holiday Pet Sleuths series!

Chapter One

"Yes. Yes, I'll be happy to take the first summer session for Gloria while she's on maternity leave. Thank you. Yes, I'll see you on Monday. I'm on campus several mornings a week this semester." Fiona finished her conversation with Dean Barclay, the head of the History and Social Sciences Department at Glencastle University. The man was very sweet but utterly clueless.

"Or maybe it's just me, Macbeth." Fiona sat back in her swiveling office chair. Macbeth, her wheat-colored Cairn Terrier, put his paws on her knee and looked up at her adoringly. "You agree?"

"Arf." Macbeth's plump little tail twitched to indicate he wholeheartedly agreed with his mistress, even if he had no idea what she was talking about.

Fiona scooped up the dog and settled him in her lap as she explained. She talked to Macbeth like he was human. After being her constant companion for so long, it was second nature. "Barclay knew I requested off for the summer. Because we were supposed to have the baby here by then, weren't we, boy?" Her voice drifted away, but for the first time in weeks, her throat didn't clog with tears. The adoption placement had fallen through. Again. Another birth mother had rejected her in favor of a two-parent family. Honestly, she bore them no ill will for that. She considered the women considering adoption for their children heroes for making a loving choice, but she also couldn't help but feel another stab of sorrow when she wasn't the one selected.

Macbeth burrowed his head under her elbow. It was clear he was saying, "Well, you still have me, Mom!"

"I know I have you, Mac. And we won't give up. Somewhere, there's a kid who needs us. Maybe a baby who is looking for a history nerd who loves dogs and chickens. But for now..." She rose before she could spend the whole afternoon sitting motionless in her chair, letting depression claim her. "But for now, it's just you and me. For now, I want to smack Barclay for asking the lady who just canceled her maternity leave because of a disrupted adoption to cover a colleague who's about to have her second set of twins. Do I sound bitter?"

Macbeth whined.

"Well. That's no good. Come on. Walk, Mac."

FIONA MILTON WAS A single, thirty-something redhead going gray. She hadn't always lived ten miles outside of Glencastle on a three-acre farmette, raising chickens and teaching online history courses while she tried to finish her doctoral dissertation that was seven years in the making.

Once, she had been married to Dr. Jordan Milton, a respected historian who was known for his VidUp lecture series, Harping on History. One day, fans started commenting that Jordan, known for his razor-sharp wit and snappy responses to questions, seemed to lose his train of thought a lot. Someone pointed out that he was always frowning as if he had a headache.

Fiona was the one who insisted he get glasses to help with his headaches and the trouble he was having with his vision. Fiona was the one who said maybe the stress of trying to finish their research together while house-hunting and trying to start a family was giving him tension headaches.

Macbeth was the one who started whining and sniffing Jordan's hair and pillow constantly as if pointing at something.

They say dogs can smell cancerous tumors in some rare cases.

But even with Macbeth's early warning system in place, Jordan hadn't responded to any treatment. The tumor was fast and vicious. After three years of marriage, Fiona was a widow at thirty. Her doctorate had been put on hold. Her dreams of motherhood hadn't seemed important in the massive tidal wave of grief that hit hard after losing Jordan.

FIONA STOPPED JUST past the chicken run. She and Macbeth shooed their little flock of ten Rhode Island Reds back into their coop for the night. Even though the days were getting longer, Fiona wanted the hens under cover before twilight, when foxes would start to prowl. She didn't worry about walking on the semi-overgrown path that led through the woods and looped back around to the front of her white and green farmhouse. At the start of the path was a weathered wooden sign that read "Jordan's Walk." Macbeth always stopped and sat there, perfectly still, while she said a little prayer and tried to think of something that Jordan would like to hear.

Today, her prayer was simply, "Help me be okay."

Forcing a smile on her face, she leaned her palm against the graying signpost. "Hey, babe. Let's see... It's the last day of Spring Break. I talked to your Mom and Dad on Easter Sunday, but I already told you that..." It was hard to find something good today, just like it had been for the past two weeks, ever since she got the call informing her she had been "unmatched."

"Oh! I know. Jordan, I got another session at the university. It's on-campus, which isn't as much fun when you want to teach history with your dog on your lap, but... guess what? It's a course on the Spice Trade and the Columbian Exchange. That'll be so much fun. Well, so much fun for history nerds like us."

Nerds like us. Us. Fiona hated to admit it to herself, but... there wasn't an "us" anymore. Jordan might be in heaven, pestering the figures from history with his questions and speculations, but she wasn't with him. What was she doing?

Talking to a piece of wood.

Living with a dog and a bunch of chickens.

Working from home whenever possible because seeing all the happy wives and husbands and all the beautiful babies with their moms and dads... was just too hard.

"Macbeth? Something has to change. I can't keep doing this. Maybe I should sell this place and move into town? Or stop trying to be a mom."

Macbeth whimpered and circled around her ankles, his blue leash wrapping around her knees. Even though Macbeth had never run off before, Fiona knew that terriers loved to chase and dig. She didn't want him tearing off after squirrels in the woods. "I'm just going in circles, boy? Yeah, no kidding."

FIONA WAS GRATEFUL that her schedule only forced her to go into Glencastle two days a week. People referred to the town as "quaint." Fiona liked it best in the summer these days. The campus emptied considerably, and the classes she taught were full of students who wanted to be there or needed the credits. Either way, they were motivated and came to class. She could also hold class outside under the massive oaks on the quad or at the picnic tables by the little creek that wove around the statue of Robert Burns.

She couldn't say the same thing about her current classes. She had a bunch of juniors and seniors scrambling to fulfill final general education requirements, and the spring semester ended in less than a month. Commencement was the Friday before Mother's Day.

"Maybe people will think I'm crying because I'm so moved by the commencement speaker's speech," Fiona scoffed to herself as she parked her SUV (also middle-aged and red going gray) in one of the reserved faculty spots in the library lot.

As full-time but "adjunct" faculty, Fiona didn't have an office to herself. She also didn't teach on campus enough to have one classroom that was always hers. There was an adjunct faculty office space in the beautiful three-story brick campus library. When she had time between classes, Fiona worked on her research, working to bolster the weak areas of her dissertation. If time ever got away from her while she was lost in her own studies, she didn't have to rush home. She could plug her laptop in at one of the half dozen desks in their beige cubicles and teach her online classes from there.

It was ideal.

Perfection.

So why hadn't she touched her dissertation in weeks?

Why did she dread taking attendance? She'd always loved children, even the teens turning into adults. She and Jordan used to spend their joint lunch hours looking at the nervous young freshman arriving for orientation, whispering what their future children would look like, wondering which majors they'd take, what instruments and sports they'd play.

"Professor Milton! Hey, Fiona! Your laptop charger!"

Fiona turned to see Dr. Sarah Weaver, one of the professors from the veterinary medicine and zoology department. She was in teal scrubs with a pawprint pattern, holding a cat carrier, a box of file folders, and nudging a white computer charger along with her foot.

"Oh, gosh! Sarah, I should be helping you carry things, not the other way around! Who's your little friend?" Fiona hurried over and retrieved her cable and wrestled the file folders away from a protesting Sarah.

"This is Bandit, my cat. Bandit's coming in to help us learn how to remove sutures."

Bandit meowed inside his carrier.

"Hey, buddy, don't complain too much. My dog *wishes* he were on campus with me. Well, no. I wish I were home with him," Fiona addressed the black and white tom in the carrier.

Sarah gave her a worried look. "You okay, babe? You seem… down."

Fiona forced a smile. "No, I'm fine." She felt like she'd asked for too much pity in the last three years. First, a wife coping with her husband's sudden illness, then as a young widow, and then as a woman going through the incredibly difficult adoption process. She felt she had no right to keep telling people her troubles. Sometimes, in an odd way, she felt like she was letting people down, all of her failures were robbing them of potential joy and good news.

Sarah stopped walking, white skid-proof sneakers crunching gravel on the walkway that led from the parking lot to the library and Seismore Hall, where the vet tech lab was located. "Do not give me that line, lady. You can't fool a vet, especially not a vet who works with horses and dogs. We're no-nonsense types."

Fiona had to admit that it was true. Sarah was not only one of her few close friends on campus, but she was also Macbeth's vet. "Right before Spring Break… another one fell through. Maybe I'm not supposed to adopt."

Sarah jostled her into a hug, plump arms squeezing her slender body into a comforting embrace. "I'm sorry, honey."

"It's okay." That's what she said now. She said it all the time. "It's okay" was an easy sounding half-truth that wasn't exactly a lie.

"Bull. *I* wouldn't be okay. It doesn't get easier just because it's happened before. Ask anyone who's ever had to put down a pet." Sarah grappled all of her baggage back into her arms while managing to keep Fiona's wrist sandwiched against her soft, comforting middle. "Not to make this worse, but… tell me something?"

"Why don't I stop?"

"Why does it have to be adoption? You're young. You could meet someone. You could turn to science, if you know what I mean."

Fiona knew what Sarah meant, but she couldn't quite work out how she wanted to respond.

"I don't know. If I ever meet someone and we have kids, that'll be great. I still think I want to adopt. Jordan and I were trying to start a family when he got diagnosed. They talked to us about how the cancer treatments might impact his ability to be a father, but because of how rapidly the mass was growing, we decided not to wait for an appointment with a fertility preservation specialist." Fiona laughed without any real joy. It was an ironic laugh. Here she was, almost four years later, telling a secret only her parents and Jordan's mother knew about. Within three minutes of entering Sarah Weaver's presence, she was spilling her guts at work on a gorgeous April day.

"I would have done the same thing. More important to fight the disease, or there wouldn't have been a future. Not that there was... Sorry, Fiona."

"It's okay." The casual lie rolled out so often she ought to have a pre-recorded message. "Anyway, we decided it must be part of God's plan. There must be a kid who really, really needed us to put Jordan through all this. To make him so sick and take away his ability to have a chance at fathering a child, God must have needed him to be a dad to someone else's baby. When..." Tears were blurring her vision now, and her steps faltered, not just because Sarah was still dragging her earnestly up the path. "When it was near the end, one of the last things Jordan said before slipping into a coma was that God's plan hadn't been about him being a dad, but me being a mom. Someone would need me as much as he needed me. Sarah, I can't do this. I can't talk about this at work. I have to look at students and talk to people. I can't go 'Oops! Technical issues' and turn my camera off." Fiona scrubbed frantically at her eyes.

"I think you need to talk to someone."

"I'm all talked out. I've done grief counseling, therapy, a widow/ widower online support group. I'm tired of talking. I want something to *happen*."

Sarah let go of her and regarded Fiona with her large gray eyes behind thin black spectacles, long gray hair frizzing out like a halo in the spring sunshine. "Then that's what I'll be praying for, sweetie."

Chapter Two

God answers prayers in very mysterious ways.

"Hey! Slow the heck down, buddy! Macbeth! Macbeth, come back!"

Monday night's walk had lasted longer than usual. She'd had a good cry driving home and another, longer, uglier crying jag out at the wooden post that bore Jordan's name. Macbeth had looked on, big brown eyes full of worry, and that had made her cry harder.

Lost in her own grief as she slowly let the day of wearing a cheerful facade fade, Fiona had almost reached the path's extreme end where it met the little-used two-lane highway that led from Glencastle to Highspire.

Suddenly, her relative calm had been shattered when a dark pickup came barreling off the road and started driving through her walking trail!

Macbeth had torn the leash from her hand and gone racing after the driver.

"He must be drunk! No way in the world would anyone think this was a road!" Fiona, knocked onto her backside, scrambled up and was jogging after Macbeth, feeling bruised and dazed. Up ahead, she could hear the truck's engine roaring and coughing as it bounced over logs and hit the leafy boughs from the trees on either side of the path. The snapping and grinding sound was horrific. Fiona didn't know whether the woods or the pickup was taking a worse beating.

Terror clutched at her heart suddenly. She guessed the driver was still going around twenty or thirty miles an hour. Macbeth couldn't catch up to them on his quick little legs, but if they stopped or swerved after slowing down ...

Lord, I can't lose Macbeth, too! This wasn't what I meant when I said I was ready for action! I was hoping You'd give, not take! "Macbeth!" Fiona whistled and called, running after him.

The sandy little terrier had stopped by the chicken coop, barking his head off. Fiona was in time to hear the engine gun and tires squeal. Speedy McIdiot had cleared the property. Judging by the deep tire gouges in the lawn, he'd swerved hard coming off of the forest path and into the (formerly) smooth lawn, slick with the cool night condensation.

"Good boy. Good boy, come." Fiona knelt and retrieved the handle of the leash, her voice shaking. She noticed her hands were shaking, too.

From fear came anger. "He could have killed you! He could have killed me! Ugh! A black truck on a dark night—of course, I didn't see the license plate." She had noted the bumper was sagging on the left side and there was some sort of red and white reflective sticker on the back of it, something with letters and numbers. Probably a parking permit for a housing complex or a workplace. Again, too dark to see anything useful. She couldn't tell the police to look for a reckless driver who had a black pickup.

"Well. Probably some foolhardy teens. I hope they got it out of their systems," Fiona tugged at the leash, trying to trick her thundering heart back to normal speed. "Macbeth. Settle. We're safe now."

But the terrier didn't settle. If anything, he became more agitated. His sharp, staccato barks were reaching the ear-splitting level he usually saved for dire emergencies, like smoke detector's beeping.

Squinting in the dark, Fiona grabbed her phone and turned on the flashlight function. A blinding dot of light appeared and she shone it around the coop. "No chickens are hurt, boy. You're a good watchdog, but I— Oh." Fiona stopped the beam short. Just beyond the deepest gouge, one that looked like it had been made by a swerving vehicle spinning its tires, was a big cooler.

But the cooler had four holes drilled into the white lid. Two bungee cords crisscrossed around the red and white body of the cooler, and it was moving.

Please, not bats. Or tarantulas. Not bats or tarantulas. Or organs. No, be sensible Fiona. Organs don't need to be kept ventilated. Or do they?

Her thumb was on the emergency call button when she heard it.

Tiny, frightened whimpers. Yipping.

Macbeth howled, something he had only done once before in his whole life.

Fiona fell to her knees and grabbed at the bungee cords. *Please don't let whatever is in here be rabid. Or deadly. Why is it locked? Why were they driving so fast?*

With a sense of dread and outrage, she lifted the lid with a wince.

"My God. Why?"

There were five tiny puppies in the box, struggling around in thick insulated blankets.

She grabbed her phone again, and this time she made a call. "Sarah!"

"Fiona?"

"Sarah, someone just careened through my lawn and dropped a cooler full of *live* puppies! Tiny, live puppies! What do I do?"

Silence.

"Sarah? Dr. Weaver?"

"I'm here. I'm delivering a foal and the phone is kind of far away. It sounded like you said someone dropped off a cooler full of puppies."

"That's what I said." As Fiona spoke, she gently gathered the puppies in the blanket and carried them to the back door. Macbeth followed at her heels, whining and panting in concern.

"Wow. Okay. Um. That's new, even for me. People are horrible."

"No kidding. What do I do? I think they were thrown—or maybe they were dropped—out of a speeding truck."

Sarah called the driver of the truck something that Fiona heartily agreed with, but it didn't solve the problem. "Can you give me an idea of how old they are?"

Fiona elbowed open the back door and put all the puppies on the warm faux-wood floor of the kitchen. Macbeth dove in, sniffing, whimpering, and nuzzling the confused, yipping puppies. Every few seconds he let out one of his high-pitched "distress" barks.

"Shh, boy, I'm here. I'm trying to get help. Sarah, I love dogs, but I'm no vet. I've never raised a litter. I have no idea how old they are." Fiona put a comforting hand on each puppy in turn, feeling their warm, wiggly little bodies. Now freed from their prison, they were tumbling over each other, unsteady on their feet. Miraculously, all of them were alive, barking, and moving. Her heart lifted slightly. If they could all move, that was a good sign, right? She looked at the blanket. No blood. A few little holes, the kind made by cigarette butts, but nothing else. No dog sick or mess.

"Just describe them. Size? Walking? Eyes open? How badly are they hurt?"

Fiona opened her mouth, but then paused, looking at the photos on the kitchen wall. There were photos of her and Jordan on their wedding day, on their various historical "research trips," and way too many pictures of Macbeth, their baby. There was a collage of him from the first photo sent by the breeder, the day they brought him home a few weeks later, and then subsequent photos up until he was two years old. Jordan had given her the collage as a Christmas gift the second year they'd had him.

"Fiona, are you there? Look, I've got to help this mare, just—"

"We got Macbeth when he was eight weeks old. Sarah, I think these are Cairn Terrier puppies! They look just like the photos we have of

Macbeth's litter. They're walking, well, *stumbling,* and they have their eyes open. None of them seem hurt."

"That's an utter miracle! Helen, move that disinfectant out of the box. Check the tail wrap, that looks a little tight. Sorry, Fiona. Look, if they're all in good shape, then they can't have traveled far. If they're walking, but not well, and their eyes are open, they're probably old enough to have puppy formula mixed with milk replacer. Ideally, they'd still be nursing."

"Right. Sure. They must have a mom somewhere. My God, who could steal baby puppies from their mothers?"

"If I think about that, I won't be taking good care of Wind Dancer. I'll call you in the morning and we'll figure this out. If they're stolen, someone probably reported it to the police. And if the pups are all in good shape after that ordeal, they weren't in their long. That means they came from nearby. Call local police and ask about missing puppies, get some milk replacer and puppy food at the Pet Market. They're open until ten. I gotta go. Oh! And look online at the college's vet page. We have a whole file of How-To sections, and one is caring for puppies and kittens who've lost their mother."

Sarah hung up.

Fiona sat for a moment, and then pulled her laptop from the kitchen island into her lap. The puppies were starting to venture off the blanket, either coming to her or Macbeth. *They're depending on me.*

Helpless babies.

Not what I envisioned when I thought of being a mother, but hey. The Lord works in mysterious ways.

Chapter Three

"Macbeth. I'm going to lock you and the kiddos in the bathroom. I know it's not ideal, but I'll bring back something better from the Pet Market. Be a good baby-sitter, okay?"

Macbeth wagged his tail once.

As soon as Fiona closed and locked the door, the cacophony of barks and whimpers started again.

Good thing I don't have neighbors.

As she sped through town, Fiona replayed the events of the last half-hour. While she'd made a list with one hand, she'd endlessly herded the puppies back to the blanket with the other, and talked to the state police, the Glencastle Police, the Highspire Police, and the police of six other towns. No one had reported missing puppies. All the police said the same thing—they would make a note of it and they'd be happy to give her the names of the local animal shelters, none of which would be open at nine at night.

Each time she said she'd keep the puppies herself, if she was allowed, and would look for the owner. The police seemed grateful that she didn't want them to get further involved, although the Glencastle Police had said they'd come out and take pictures of her vandalized property. They also said that without some sort of identifying marks or a license number, they probably couldn't find the reckless driver.

"Could the driver be the owner of the dogs? Surely someone would report five puppies stolen! Especially if they're purebred, and I think they are. There was easily between five and ten thousand dollars in that cooler!" Fiona ranted.

But the thoughts of how and why the puppies were in that container and why the driver was speeding through a forest like a maniac wouldn't help keep the puppies alive. True, she'd locked them in the bathroom with Macbeth (who was a great guard dog, despite his small size) to keep them from destroying her house, but also because she hoped to keep them safe from the mysterious dognapper—if he existed.

"I shouldn't have left them alone. Jordan, if you were still here, you'd run to the store and I'd watch the puppies. Or maybe you'd stay home and guard them, the man of the house, the big Papa Bear." Fiona winked at the roof of the car, a tight smile on her face.

At the Pet Market, she bought a big puppy enclosure, which looked like a giant expanding fence, a bunch of piddle pads and a washable puppy enclosure mat, way too many toys, and a bunch of puppy milk replacer and food. She also bought Macbeth a box of gourmet dog biscuits because she didn't want him to feel left out.

As Fiona swiped her credit card and winced at the total, she realized she'd probably be taking all of this back the next day. Surely someone would report the puppies missing by then.

"I PICTURED... SETTING up a crib. Ugh! And 3 AM feedings. Eww. Macbeth, stop. One, two, three, four... where's five? Macbeth! Where's Puppy Number Five?"

Fiona stopped struggling to set up the "easy assembly" puppy enclosure. It had already banged her in the shins and funny bone, and while she was trying to avoid getting another bump, she noticed another puppy puddle on the laminate wood flooring of the farmhouse's open, airy kitchen. She had planned to keep the puppies in there, close enough to check on, but far enough away from her desk that they wouldn't be overheard by her students.

"I have to start calling you something besides numbers, too," Fiona muttered as she stopped her work to search for the missing pup. The puppies, even though they were wiggly and weak, seemed to be good at evading her. It was the plump little pup with the darkest fur that had wandered off. Macbeth sniffed him out and returned him (or her) to the fold by nudging him along.

With a grunt, Fiona snapped the last piece of the enclosure into place and stepped over the fence. She dragged the bedding and piddle pads over and began making up this temporary shelter.

"It wouldn't be so bad if it wasn't temporary." Fiona blew a strand of hair from her forehead as she watched Macbeth nuzzling and pushing the puppies back to where he felt they should be, whimpering worriedly all the while. "Aw, Mac. I'm sorry, buddy." Fiona knew it was silly, but she was suddenly overwhelmed with guilt. After Jordan's death, she'd shut herself off, entombing herself in her comfort zone, and taking Macbeth with her. He'd probably missed other dogs. Maybe he would have found a nice lady terrier and had a family of his own by now if she hadn't been so reluctant to get back to the land of the living.

"Hey, Mac. Mac, when we find out who owns these little guys, I bet the owner will be grateful. Dr. Weaver can vouch for us. We'll adopt one of these pups and you can have a friend, okay?" Fiona spoke in a soft, soothing voice as she put the finishing touches on the enclosure.

Macbeth sat on his haunches as she lifted each squirming puppy over the fence. When the last pup was over, Macbeth put his paws up against the plastic gate and whined, thick feather of a tail twitching impatiently. "You want to sleep in here with the babies? You old softie." Fiona lifted him over, her heart melting at how adorable the sight of her terrier and his surrogate litter was.

Adoption for the win... but this isn't right. I'm convinced these puppies have a good home somewhere, and probably a frantic mother and father.

After watching the puppies settle into the nest of old towels she'd made, Fiona decided she'd better sleep downstairs. Shaking her head and whispering, "I'm overdoing it. I'm getting too involved..." Fiona dragged her air mattress over and stationed herself on the floor of the kitchen, right next to the enclosure.

"Good night, everyone. Don't worry. We'll get everything straightened out, tomorrow."

Chapter Four

After a hasty breakfast and a test run of her least favorite new sport, "Puppy Poop Pick Up", Fiona dragged the enclosure, her laptop, and a patio chair out into the warm April sun. She could grade papers, keep an eye on the pups, and wait for the police to come and photograph the tire ruts in her lawn.

"You guys are lucky it's Tuesday. Tomorrow I have class on campus. You'll have to stay inside—well, if you're still here." Fiona bit her lip and reached down over the gate to pick up a whimpering brindle-coated pup. As the puppy nibbled her fingers, she opened her laptop and searched "Vets in Castle County."

"Ughhh." A groan escaped her lips as the results loaded. "Let's narrow it down. We'll start with vets in Glencastle and Highspire."

"HI. LOOK, I'VE ALREADY made a dozen calls, but I'm hoping you can help me. The police and Dr. Sarah Weaver, professor of veterinary medicine at Glencastle University, suggested I call you." Fiona sat stiffly on the edge of the plastic chair, her voice firm and her fingers crossed. After the first two vets had told her that they couldn't give out any patient information, even in a good cause, Fiona had decided to bend the rules. The police and Dr. Weaver had suggested various methods of handling the sudden influx of baby canines, and she would loosely interpret their words as needed.

There was a pause on the receiving end of the call. "Oh. Uh. Sure. What can we help you with?" asked an uncertain voice.

"Some malicious prankster stole a litter of terrier puppies. I'm fairly certain they are Cairn Terriers."

"My gosh. You'd better call the police!"

"No, they're not *my* puppies. I found them in my yard after they were stolen. Borrowed. Whatever."

"Well, then the person who had them stolen should call the police!"

Fiona counted to ten as she closed her eyes. "I agree. But since word hasn't reached the police—yet—this is something I'm doing to assist them. Do any of your patients have a pregnant terrier? Or rather, one that was due?"

"I'll ask Dr. Masterson."

Cheerful hold music assaulted her tired ears.

"Hey. Dr. Masterson says we can't give you that information unless the police call us first. You can have them call us and then we'll call you."

Fiona stared at her phone as it beeped. She'd been hung up on.

"Okay. This is an emergency. I'm going to have to get drastic." Fiona looked at Macbeth with pursed lips, and moved onto the next phone number.

"Highspire Veterinary Clinic, how may we help you?"

"Well, I was hopin' you could help me with a problem I've been havin'!" Fiona drawled in a Southern accent that would have put Scarlet O'Hara to shame. She had to bite down a laugh as Macbeth sniffed at her ankles and gave a single worried whine as if to say, "First all these puppies arrive, and now my human is broken, too?!"

"I hope we can help you. Are you a returning patient?"

Fiona's eyebrows arched on her own. She'd thought an accent like that would be memorable in this area! However, she pressed on with a dramatic sigh, "No, I'm not a patient, I'm a brokenhearted woman. You see, my husband just passed and he was so awful fond of dogs. Terriers, mostly. His favorite breed was the Cairn Terrier." All of this was strictly true. Fiona thought Jordan would approve of helping her with this ruse and she was able to smile as she said, "I'd just love to get a Cairn Terrier pup to keep me company and to honor his memory. Problem is, I can't seem to find anyone in these here parts with a litter. Would y'all happen to know of a local breeder or even an individual with a litter that might be willin' to sell a pup when the time is right?"

"Ooh, you're in luck. Cairns aren't one of the 'trendy' breeds, but they're so adorable. We do have a family who raises Cairns and Westies. Wells' Westies and Cairns. I can give you the name of their website? All of the information about upcoming litters should be on it."

Fiona did a little victory jig in her lawnchair, nearly tipping backward. "Thank you!" she squealed, her accent vanishing.

Macbeth gave a sigh and laid down next to his adopted litter.

"THE WELLS HOMESTEAD and Studio." Fiona tapped in the address that the receptionist had given her, crossing her fingers as the page loaded.

"Wow." Wells' Westies and Cairns was more than just a site for dog breeders. The tabs across the top of the page instantly showed that the Wells were a multi- talented couple. "Listen, Mac. Carving and Sculpting. Gift shop. Studio. Kennel. Homestead Produce." Fiona looked around her own yard. Chickens. Flowers. Puppies—which were temporary.

She and Jordan would have loved to have that kind of lifestyle. They wouldn't be sculpting and painting. They'd be reading and researching, sitting side by side while their kids picked apples and fed the chickens. Her heart squeezed hard. To distract herself, she quickly hit the tab for the kennel.

"Bingo!" Fiona cheered as she saw a photo of wriggly-looking puppies under a banner that proclaimed "March Litter—Purebred Cairns," she read aloud, "The perfect Spring Surprise for Mom! Puppies ready to go around Mother's Day. Look…" Fiona squinted at the photo of—"Yes! one, two, three, four, five!"

This has to be the same litter, Fiona thought, scanning the tumbling, whining bundles at her feet. There were many things that could change about a newborn pup's appearance, but this litter had a mix of brindle and dark gray pups. There was only one pup in the photo that was almost black, and the same held true of her overnight guests. "Bingo," she whispered, sighing in relief.

With a hand that was shaking from exhaustion, Fiona dialed the number on the website.

After five rings, a soft, steady feminine voice greeted her. It was the sort of voice just made for giving step-by-step instructions on how to make bread or change a flat tire, but Fiona didn't find herself soothed by it.

"You've reached the Wells' Homestead, Studio, and Kennel. If you're calling to inquire about our pups, please press one."

Fiona jabbed one, tension running down her spine. This had to be the right place! Why weren't they camped by the phone, waiting for news? Maybe they were on the other line with the police.

Or maybe the dognappers called and demanded a fraudulent ransom! The knot of tension turned into a hot spike.

"Blake and Peggy can't come to the phone right now. But if you leave a message, we'll get back to you in two shakes of a Westie's tail!"

"Nauseating," Fiona muttered as a melodic scale indicated she should start speaking. "Hi, my name is Fiona. I think I have your missing litter. Assuming that your litter is missing, that is." Sweat suddenly made her palms slippery as she balanced the phone against her cheek. *What if they think I stole their puppies? Is it possible they haven't discovered the theft yet?* "Uh. Let me try again." Her voice wobbled. "I think you have a bunch of missing Cairn Terrier puppies, and I have them. I didn't *take* them, but they were dropped in my yard. Uh. Call me back."

It was only after she hung up that Fiona realized she hadn't left her number.

"Oh, well. They'll call me back. I'm sure their answering system collects the caller's numbers." She sank back in her chair.

It had been nice having someone need her for a little bit. And Macbeth had been happy (if worried) by the influx of canine company.

In the spring sunshine, Fiona closed her eyes and listened to the soft noises of puppies at play and blocked out the ugly gouges the speeding truck had made in her lawn.

Well. I prayed to stop going in circles. I prayed for something to happen. I was hoping it would be a human baby, but okay, God. I'll take a puppy.

At least I would... if the Wells would call me back!

Chapter Five

Fiona's face was flaming, and with her red hair, it wasn't a good look. "I'm a tomato with a bun," she grunted and glared at the rearview mirror.

Twenty-four hours had passed. She had a copy of the police report. She'd had Sarah Weaver come and examine the puppies and make a few calls. All the scanty threads of information seemed to wind their back to the Wells family.

And what didn't she have?

A return call from Blake and Peggy Wells, who were now coming across as very different people in Fiona's mind. Instead of being the wronged owners, frantically searching for their missing litter, now she was wondering if they were crooked puppy mill breeders, or if they were involved in something shady and they'd dumped the puppies on purpose.

It made her angrier and angrier as she caught every light on the way back from campus to her house. Her face felt hot enough to cook a steak.

"How is this fair? Why does this keep happening? People don't appreciate what they have."

Like the women in their perfect suits with their huge diamond rings by the coffee maker in the faculty lounge, whining about how annoying it was to have a third child to drag to sports practice or a second baby on the way...

They're allowed to vent, honey. That's what Jordan would have told her, in his patient voice that used to make her so mad... and now she missed it.

"Okay, okay. People can vent. Venting is fine. It's not fine to throw away innocent puppies like garbage." Fiona screeched around a curve and roared out onto the country road that led to her house.

She had an idea brewing, and ideas that came to her when she was riled up weren't usually her best.

And nowadays Jordan wasn't there to talk her down off that ledge.

Fiona stormed into the kitchen when she got home, letting the screen door slam behind her. "Macbeth! Puppies! Come on, little guys. I'm going to take you home."

IT WASN'T UNTIL SHE was turning onto Wicker Hill Road, following beautiful hand-painted signs that proclaimed "Wells Homestead and Studio" that her common sense started kicking back in.

What if something really bad had happened to Blake and Peggy? Maybe they'd had a horrible accident and couldn't return the call. What if they were on vacation or something? She'd look like a lunatic if she showed up screaming with a basket of puppies in tow.

"Oh, well. I'm here now. I should at least try to make contact." Fiona parked, cracked the windows so the dogs could enjoy the fresh spring air, and climbed out of the car.

For a homestead and studio, the place looked...quiet. She had pictured milling animals and the noises of artisans and crafting. Where were the Westies and Cairns promised on the website?

Her stomach clenched. Something didn't feel right about the place.

Fiona reached for the pepper spray on her keychain and swiped up on her phone screen, ready to call for help.

The smart thing to do would be get back in the car.

But what if the Wells are lying in there, hurt?

Oh, God? If you're not too busy, I could use a little help. I'm torn between being brave and being safe. What do I do? A little sign would be nice.

"Nn! Nnnnn!"

Fiona whipped around. Over on the enclosed porch behind the white picket fence was a single terrier, its paws up on the screen.

Fiona's feet moved on their own, marching with long strides to the front of the rambling wooden farmhouse where she hammered at the door. "Mr. Wells? Mrs. Wells? Blake! Peggy!"

Footsteps thundered toward the front door almost at once. Fiona took a hasty step back and put her finger on the catch of her pepper spray—just in case.

"Who is it?" A deep voice demanded from behind the closed door adorned with a wicker wreath.

"Fiona! The lady who left the message. I have something I need to give to Mr. and Mrs. Wells!" Fiona shouted through the door.

A shrill chorus of staccato barking erupted inside the house. From the long dirt driveway, Macbeth and the pups gave their best retort, howling and yapping.

"We don't want any."

"What? You don't even know what I have!" Fiona kicked the bottom of the door and sucked in a deep breath. "Look, I've been told you have a litter of Cairns. I found a litter of Cairns. I think—"

"Not ours! The mother lost the litter. Pregnancy complications. Go away or I'm going to call the police."

"Why don't you try it, buddy?" Fiona growled, slamming the flat of her hand against the door. "But if you want to sell that lie, you might ought to take down the puppy pictures off your website!"

There was silence and then the sound of a chain rattling against the wood.

Fiona bit her lip and prepared to flee or fight—only to find herself looking at salt and pepper hair, deep brown eyes, and an outdoorsman's tanned face. "Mr. Wells?"

"Look, we got the message. But the answer hasn't changed." His harsh voice suddenly thickened. "You can go with whatever you've got."

With a squint of confusion, Fiona shook her head. "What I've got? I've got your puppies, you jerk! Some madman flung them out of a truck! If you don't want them back, then say so. Or better yet, give me the mother dog! These puppies aren't fully weaned, and if that's what you do to helpless babies, I can't imagine what you're doing to their poor mother!"

With a clank, Mr. Wells tore open the door, sending the little brass chain swinging. "You found them?"

Fiona resisted the urge to smack him and smacked her forehead instead. "I left you a message, *and* I just said that! You're the one who—whoop!" Fiona found herself tugged inside the farm house by a firm hand on her elbow.

Mr. Wells slammed the door and then leaned against the wall, his knees sagging and his head hanging low. "Oh, thank God. I thought you were with them."

This time, Fiona's stomach clenched in a way she hadn't experienced since before Jordan died. There was a puzzle to solve here, some secret to unravel.

"I'm not with anyone but a bunch of sad puppies and a very nervous Cairn Terrier who wasn't prepared to become a dad overnight."

Blake Wells looked up at her and gave her a woebegone smile. "Yeah. Me, neither. That's kind of how I got into this mess, Miss—"

"Fiona. Fiona Milton."

Blake hesitated, then stuck out his hand. "Well, you're in the house now. I'm warning you, I've got carpentry tools and I'm not afraid to use them."

Fiona backed up a step, yanking her hand free. "I'll be happy to leave if that's the case!"

Blake shook his head. "No. I'm sorry—I'm just... I'm just warning you that if this is an act and you're trying to take her, you'll have to get through me and a sledgehammer first!"

"Take who?" Fiona blurted, one hand on the doorknob.

"Daddy! Nap over!"

Fiona and Blake's eyes turned to the top of the stairs where a bright little face with a shock of red hair peeped over a toddler gate.

"Her," Blake said grimly. "Coming, sweetie."

"Biscuit's cryin'." The toddler pointed downstairs, her chubby fist waving.

Fiona realized that one dog was still making a particularly mournful yip every few seconds. "Is Biscuit a mommy dog?" Fiona called out as Blake climbed the stairs.

"Yes!" the little one called, sounding very proud of herself. "Who dat? Daddy, who dat?"

"I don't know yet, baby. Someone who might make Biscuit feel better. Uh, lady? If you have what you said, do you want to go get them? Or were you looking for a reward?"

Fiona sniffed out an angry huff, the best she could manage in front of innocent ears. "No, I was trying to do the right thing. Last time I checked, that's a free service!"

Fiona marched back to her car, clipped Macbeth's leash to his collar, then herded all the puppies into the large, sturdy laundry basket she'd been using to carry them en masse.

I hope I'm doing the right thing.

Fiona's steps quickened. She might be annoyed at Mr. Wells' attitude and frustrated by the confusion and accusations he'd levied, but her stomach was still tingling in anticipation.

"Onward, Macbeth."

Chapter Six

Biscuit was a pretty little wheaten-colored Cairn Terrier, and her joy at being reunited with her babies made Fiona reach for a tissue. When Blake told her Macbeth could hang out with the mother and pups on the porch, all (okay, most of) her annoyance at the man melted.

"Won't her mate get angry?" Fiona asked, one hand still clasping the phone inside her pocket in case things went south.

"No. Sadly. Peanut Butter—the father—crossed the Rainbow Bridge right after he and Biscuit—uh, started this family." Blake gave a toddler-friendly explanation as he put down two glasses of lemonade and a sippy cup on the large wooden table that faced the porch. "He was young, too. Stomach cancer."

"Cancer is evil." Fiona crossed her arms and sat reluctantly.

"Who's dat? Who's dat?" The toddler continued her chant as she waddled back from the little bathroom off the kitchen.

"I'm Fiona. I found Biscuit's puppies." Fiona smiled at the little girl and watched her smile back, a sprinkle of tiny freckles across her nose wrinkling up as she grinned.

"Hey, sweetie, do you want to go visit the puppies? Take your juice and be careful. Is Macbeth good with kids?" Blake asked, holding the little one's hand and helping her down the step to the enclosed porch at the back of the house.

"He is. He's a good family dog." Fiona felt her eyes mist again. Macbeth was supposed to be playing with the child and she and Jordan would have had, or if not that, the baby she had been chosen to adopt before that adoption fell through.

"Is he our dog, Daddy?"

"No, honey bunny. He's a visiting doggie."

Blake settled the little girl with her juice and a bunch of tug toys for the puppies. "She's very gentle and so is Biscuit."

"I can see that. So. Want to tell me what in the world is going on?"

Blake drained his lemonade. "Not really."

"Well, you asked if I wanted to be paid, and I do. In information. I like to research, and this is something I'm curious about."

Blake looked around warily and ran his work-roughened hand back through his wavy bangs. "Lady, if you want to know, I'll tell you, but you're probably going to regret it. Trust me, you don't want to be in the middle of this. I think you should take your dog and leave."

Fiona felt generations of Scotch-Irish stubbornness clamoring to be unleashed. "No. I think it sounds like you need help. And frankly, you're lucky I didn't have a cooler of dead puppies to return to you. If you're in the middle of something, it must be something bad, because only really horrible, desperate people would wrap puppies up like burritos, shove 'em in a cooler, and drive at ninety miles an hour through the woods until the cooler fell off in my yard!"

Blake gasped and began to rise from his chair—but then fell back. "My Lord! I had no idea it was that bad. This is so terrible, I—"

"But you were going to just let me keep them!" Fiona pointed out. "You knew someone stole them! Why didn't you call the police? Why didn't—"

Blake cut her off with a sharp whisper, "If it was a choice between the puppies or Hannah, I knew what I had to do!"

"The puppies or Hannah?" Fiona's eyes swiveled to the redheaded little girl now giggling as three puppies tried to lick animal cracker crumbs off her cheeks. "That's her?"

"Yeah, Hannah is my foster child—and I'm due to adopt her right around Mother's Day." Blake's face lit up and Fiona had to remind herself that Blake was a married man and she wasn't interested in romance.

But when he smiled, a dead zone in her brain seemed to come to life and remember that while Jordan was gone—*she* was still here and people sometimes got a second chance at happiness.

"That's great news. I'm happy for you."

"Well, some other people aren't, including a Mr. Reyes."

"A lawyer?"

"The man who claims to be her biological father."

"Ah. He wants Hannah back, I presume?" Fiona's brows drew together in confusion. "Well, threatening you and stealing your dogs isn't going to make the foster care system look favorably upon him! And you have nothing to do with her placement."

Blake shrugged. "I could withdraw my petition to adopt her. If he's the biological father, my attorney says I might lose in a court battle, anyway." The deep brown eyes closed and his head tipped back, resting on the ladderback of the wooden dining room chair.

"If he's the father?" Fiona pressed. "Do you mean there's some doubt?"

Blake opened one eye slowly. "Are you sure you're not from his gang?"

"Gang? Me?" Fiona was mortified and flattered at the same time. "I'm not in any gang. Don't you think I'm a little old for that?"

"I dunno. What are you, twenty-five? Thirty?" Blake shrugged and didn't wait for an answer. "You just dug right to the root of it, that's all."

"I told you, I'm a researcher. We cut through the crap."

That got a small chuckle out of the man. Blake spent a long moment looking at his foster daughter and then turned to Fiona. "All right, professor, here's the story."

"I actually *am* a professor," Fiona grinned. " I work at Glencastle University."

This time Blake's laugh was a little stronger, but not by much. "Funny how these things keep happening. Almost like—well, never mind. Mr. Reyes wasn't around until a few months ago. Hannah remembers her mother, but she doesn't recognize him at all, and certainly not as her Daddy. But that's not the most worrying thing. Mr. Reyes is Hispanic, with dark hair and eyes. And *this* is a picture of Hannah's mother." Blake snatched a photo from the fridge and held it out.

Fiona examined the photo of Hannah in the arms of a dark haired, blue-eyed woman with pale, creamy skin and Hannah's freckled nose. The shape of the face, the eye-color, and the freckles were identical. So was the fair skin, although Fiona noticed that the young woman's arms were dark in places and her eyes were quite sunken.

"Heroin. It didn't start that way. She was a college athlete who had a bad back injury. Got doped up. Couldn't get off the painkillers. Couldn't feel better without 'em. You know how it ended. Same way it ends for a lot of beautiful people." Blake put the photo back on the fridge with a reverent pat. "You tell me where Hannah's red hair comes from if both parents have dark brown hair."

Fiona pursed her lips. "I'm sorry Hannah has suffered so much loss at such a young age. As for Mr. Reyes, maybe he was an absentee father who feels like he has to step up now that there isn't another parent in the picture? It's very rare, but it *is* possible to have two brunette parents and a redheaded child. It's a matter of recessive genes."

Blake waved her words away impatiently. "Reyes calls her Anna. Not Hannah."

"Oh, could you have misheard? It happens with—" Fiona stopped playing devil's advocate as another paper from the fridge landed in her lap.

Fiona unfolded a dirt-streaked piece of paper.

"That was folded up on the windshield of my truck last week."

Anna is my daughter. You'll be in a world of trouble if you don't get that. Bring her to me or I'll come take her.

"Mr. Wells! Blake, this is serious! Call the police." Fiona dropped the paper to the table between them.

"I did. They said it's very concerning, a great big threat—to someone. According to the police, it might not be for me. It doesn't mention my name or Hannah's name, and the note was left on the car in a huge strip mall parking lot. Because there isn't any direct evidence, they say there isn't anything they can do. It could have been meant for anyone—but I know it wasn't. Hannah isn't Reyes' daughter, and if he was her real father, he'd know I can't just hand her over. He wants her for some reason, and I'm not gonna let that creep get his mitts on her!"

"What about the foster care system?"

Blake rubbed his eyes, a weary spasm crossing his scruffy jaw. "There's no official father on record in their system. Hannah's mother was a single parent. Sure, there's a father someplace, maybe even a real great guy... but he either didn't know about Hannah or didn't care to take responsibility for her." Blake lowered his voice and leaned over. Fiona followed suit, a strange thrill running up her arm as he whispered to her, "There were no child support documents, no letters and cards, and I can't get access to her birth certificate yet. I've been approved to legally adopt her, but like I said, Mr. Reyes could challenge that."

"Could? Don't you know if he is?" Fiona whispered back.

Blake shook his head. "He came to the house and said he was going to—but he hasn't filed anything legal that I know of. When I contacted the case worker, she said all birth certificates were managed by the state system, and I would have to go through them. They called back and said that I'll have to wait until the adoption is finalized in May, fill out the proper forms, and then in six months I will get a copy of her birth certificate and updated records where I'll be listed as her legal parent."

"But in the meantime, can't you and Mrs. Wells report what Reyes has been doing? Put a camera on the property and catch him making threats? Then you could bring this to a head."

Blake froze and backed away. There was an anger in his eyes that quickly flared and then died out, replaced by sadness. "Single father. Widower."

Fiona clapped a hand to her mouth. "Oh! Oh, my goodness. I'm so sorry. I saw the website and I thought—"

"I still sell her work. Peggy made this place what it is. I can't bear to take her photos off the website yet. A lot of people don't understand—it's been almost a year now, but—"

"Believe me. I understand. My husband died three years ago. I still—hrm—still talk to him every day," Fiona admitted with a blush. She waited for the mocking look to come across Blake's face, but instead, he nodded.

"I talk to Peggy every night. Especially about Hannah. We'd been in the foster-to-adopt program through our church's orphan advocacy ministry. When Peggy... When Peggy was in an accident, I wasn't eligible anymore. They only wanted two parent families, and they said that maybe I was grieving and wouldn't be a good fit. Well, the state felt differently. They're desperate for parents. When they found out I worked from home and had a home study completed, they put Hannah with me. That was four months ago, and it's been the best thing ever." The craftsman's face lit up. "Did you and your late husband have children?"

"No. We tried." Fiona coughed. "That is, we were thinking about trying when they found the tumor. It was so fast. So aggressive. Treatment options would destroy Jordan's fertility, but we didn't have any time to waste. For us, it wasn't a big decision. We'd always talked about adoption, anyway." Fiona grabbed her lemonade and sipped, chugging it too fast in an attempt to undo the lump in her throat. Instead, she spluttered, gagged, and a lemon seed came flying out of her nose. Hearing his human mother in distress, Macbeth came barreling in and stood between her and Blake, emitting a low warning growl.

"Mac, stop. Mommy is fine. Mommy is just a little mortified," Fiona gagged, the tart juice making her eyes water. "Lemonade is better ingested than used to irrigate the sinuses."

"Daddy! Can we keep the new doggy?" Hannah came crawling out of the puppy zone and plopped down next to Macbeth. Macbeth snorted at Blake, looked at Fiona, and then flopped across the toddler's lap.

"No, sweetie."

"Pweeease?" Hannah stuck out her lower lip and wrapped her arms around the unprotesting dog.

Fiona melted. She watched Blake's face shift, too, his lips twitching. It was clear he would love to say yes. *That little girl has him wrapped around her finger.*

And it's very endearing.

"Macbeth is Miss Fiona's puppy. She would miss him. She would be sad without him. We can't take him."

Hannah paused, then nodded solemnly, lower lip going back to its normal little rosebud shape. "Can he come play?"

"Yes. If he's invited back," Fiona spoke up quickly.

"I think that's possible. Hannah, do you want to give Macbeth a dog cookie? Go get him one from the porch. Give one to Biscuit, too."

"Cookies! Cookies, puppy, come on!" She squealed and ran, which caused Macbeth to yip and romp after her.

"He's a great dog. Is he intact?"

Fiona nodded, blushing for some reason.

"Would you ever consider letting him stud? I'd pay good fees."

"Uh—I'll think about it. Isn't there a more pressing problem? What are you going to do about Reyes and Hannah?"

"Wait him out. He's started to escalate things by breaking into the outdoor kennel and kidnapping the puppies. It was him or an associate,

I know it. Hannah and I were just at the store for thirty minutes or so. When I came back, Biscuit was running around the yard, barking her head off. If we'd been home, I'd hate to think what he might've tried..." Blake's face hardened. "But he's a coward. Reyes won't come at me, he'll come at something helpless and see if he can get me to crack. Those dogs are a lot of income and I love 'em, but if it was a question between Hannah and the puppies, like I told you, there's no question."

"You could report this to the police!"

"There's no proof he did it. I don't have cameras on the property—yet. Everything would be my word against his, and for all I know, the cops would think this place wasn't safe for Hannah and—and I'd lose her." Blake's voice cracked suddenly. With a cough, he pressed on. "I know he's involved in something shady. He offered me *cash* for Hannah. I paid one of those websites $29.99 to see his criminal record and he has a busy rapsheet—all for violence or minor possession of illegal substances. But it also said he works at a car wash in Glencastle. How does a guy working at a car wash have the kind of money he was offering me? It was a *lot*— but Hannah is priceless. So, based on Hannah's history, here's my theory." Blake stopped abruptly. "Why am I telling you all this?"

Fiona blew her nose (which stung) and crossed her arms. "I'm a good guy. Every hero needs a sidekick. You're the hero for trying to save Hannah. I'm the sidekick. I rescued the puppies. Now our paths have crossed."

"Doesn't that make us both heroes in different comic strips?"

"Well, consider this a special crossover edition."

Blake's smile stretched, quirking up at one corner to show teeth that seemed extra bright against his tan face. "I love a woman who uses comic book logic. Okay. To quote the greats, 'Avengers assemble!' My theory is that Reyes knew Hannah's mother, and maybe Hannah's father. They might have all run with the same crowd or gang. Reyes could have been her dealer. My hunch is that there is something he thinks he can get if he has Hannah. Not something out of me, because I'd already give everything I own for that little girl. So who does that leave?"

"Maternal grandparents?"

"None."

"Paternal grandparents?"

"If he was the dad, why would he need a grandkid to influence his own parents? My money is on Hannah's real father. If I could find him and get him to agree to a DNA test or agree to sign over his parental rights, Reyes would have no case."

Fiona felt that eager tingling in her stomach and spine intensify. This was a mystery. This was a real case. Even better, it was a modern mystery, one she could solve in person, not by using ancient volumes and endless hours in libraries or on archaeological digs. But it was also worse. Real people in real time meant real danger, and one currently living, very much alive little girl was hanging in the balance.

"What are you going to do? How can you find him?"

"I'm going to look for clues in Hannah's mother's belongings, which were left to Hannah and I have custody of at the moment, and then I'll look up Reyes' associates. Maybe I can find names of people he was arrested with or in connection with."

"That sounds time consuming. Don't you have to work?"

Blake shrugged. "I'll hire a private detective if I have to."

Fiona nodded. An offer was forming at the edge of her lips, but her common sense told her to keep silent.

I've had enough of you, she informed her brain. *No more thinking. Action!*

"Hire me. I mean, don't *hire* me, use me! I mean—no. Allow me to help you." Fiona rose and tried to look as sane and competent as possible. Maybe God would temporarily remove Mr. Wells' memory of the angry tomato pounding on his door or the woman who shot lemonade out of her nose and all over her pants.

"Uh... You've helped a lot! You found the dogs. And maybe if the police investigated what happened with the speeding truck in your yard, we can get some strings together that will tie up Reyes!" Blake seized her elbows and shook them in his excitement.

He had a noticeably strong grip, which was completely immaterial and not worth noticing.

So why was she noticing?

"Yes! They did! I have a police report! Maybe we can find out what kind of car Reyes drives!"

"Exactly. That would be a big help."

"But I can do more. I'm a researcher. I unravel hundred-year-old mysteries. I can help find Hannah's dad. I have access to state databases through my university subscriptions. I'm not supposed to use them for anything but my own research, but I'll make up a good reason. I could say I was testing the efficacy of the system when applied to a modern situation."

Blake looked blank, then nodded. "Yes, you could. But you don't have to. I can pay you, but I think I'd rather hire a professional."

"Hire a professional, then. Still let me help!" Fiona begged. She didn't know why this was so important to her... only she did.

A widow and widower.

An adoption on the verge of falling through.

A child to help.

Even the same kind of dog and the same big, ramshackle farmhouse that was heavy on clutter and warmth and light on organization.

"I had an adoption fall through this month. I know what it's like to know you could lose someone who wasn't even 'yours' to love, but you loved them. You loved them before you even met them. And I know what it's like to love someone who isn't even here anymore when people are telling you to move on. I know what it's like to worry about going on alone." Her voice was a rough rasp, and she coughed before saying brightly, "And what's more, I work from home part-time. Your late wife had a studio, right?"

Blake nodded, eyes roving over all the examples of their handiwork scattered around the interior of the house. "She was a potter. She did clay. I do wood."

"I bet it would help to have someone watch Hannah and the dogs in case Reyes or anyone else tries anything sinister. I could use Peggy's studio—just for a couple of weeks until we find Hannah's biological father or enough evidence to get Reyes out of the picture some other way. Please. I... I know it sounds pathetic, but I have been *praying* for God to give me some direction, some action to take because I'm just spinning my wheels. Maybe if I help someone else get pushed out of the metaphorical ditch, I'll be next." Fiona smiled at him hopefully, knowing her eyes must be glistening and her nose was probably bright pink, because it always got pink just before the tears started to flow.

Blake's lips thinned, and then he turned away. He put his hands on the faded granite worktop of the center kitchen island and let out a deep, rattling sigh. "You wanna know something crazy?"

"It seems to fit the situation," Fiona answered, stepping closer.

"I've been praying for God to send someone to watch my back. I thought He was going to send a state trooper or a social worker. Not a professor with a basket of puppies."

Fiona winced. She wasn't sure if this was leading to a refusal or a compliment. "Maybe I'm enough?"

"Daddy! Can Biscuit and Macbeth get married if I find a bowtie?" Hannah shouted, interrupting the tense moment.

Blake laughed. "Maybe you're perfect. Uh—you'd better go. My daughter is playing matchmaker."

Fiona left his side to join the toddler and the puppies. *Jordan, what's happening? This wasn't the way things were supposed to go! I was supposed to return the puppies and leave, not commit myself to helping indefinitely!* Fiona found herself looking skyward as she talked to her "guardian angel."

"What's matchmaker? Can we play it?" Hannah demanded, clapping her hands as Fiona bent down to scritch Biscuit behind the ears.

"It's not exactly a game. It's when someone helps two people find each other so they can be together. Like sweethearts."

"Like daddies and mommies?"

"Right. Like that. Hannah... do you know your daddy's name?"

"Bwake."

"Do you know if your mommy had any friends? Sweethearts?"

"Me. I was her sweetie. But now I'm Daddy's sweetie." Hannah laid down next to Biscuit and grabbed a puppy to hug. She handled the little animal carefully and gently, and Biscuit looked on without a single grunt.

"I know you are."

"Can you have more than one sweetie? Can you be the sweetie of two people?" Hannah asked, kicking off one of her socks.

Fiona retrieved it and reflexively put it back on. "I guess so. Like Biscuit's puppies. They're her sweeties and your sweeties."

Hannah nodded. She rocked her head back and forth, eyes going hazy and dreamy. "Are you gonna be here when I wake up?"

"I don't know. But I'll come back."

"'Kay."

Fiona watched the eyes close, and eased away, silently beckoning to Macbeth.

As she turned to leave, she heard a soft, sleepy mumble. "Mommy loves me. An' Daddy loves me. Jesus loves me. Biscuit. Puppies. Tyler."

Fiona turned back. "Tyler?"

Hannah nodded in her half-asleep state. "Mommy's other sweetie."

Fiona turned so quickly that she almost screamed when she collided with Blake's solid chest. "Oh! Sorry."

"She does this sometimes. She takes a nap and a half," he smiled.

"Who's Tyler?"

"Huh? I don't know. Why?"

"She said Mommy's sweetie is Tyler."

"Tyler?" Blake repeated.

"Is it a cartoon character? Stuffed animal?"

Blake shook his head.

Fiona felt like jumping. "There were no siblings, were there?"

"No, just her."

"Blake, what if Tyler is Hannah's father?"

Chapter Seven

Nice as her offer was, Blake didn't take Fiona up on it without exercising some caution. He made her wait, one eye warily on her, one eye on a laptop with a cracked and sticker-covered case. "I paid for a three-month membership to FindPeopleZone. I might as well use it," Blake said with a guilty half-chuckle.

Fiona nodded, pacing. Hannah was still asleep on the enclosed porch that was attached to the kitchen, the April breezes bringing in the scent of flowers and farmlife. Through the shady screened porch, she could see the kennels beyond the house where two Westies were playing. She wondered if this had once been a bigger operation, with more dogs. Had things scaled down once Blake's wife died?

Her plans—herck, her whole world—had shrunk after Jordan died. Or maybe fostering Hannah was taking up the bulk of his time.

"My gosh! You're Jordan Milton's wife!" Blake shouted.

On the porch, Biscuit and Macbeth, who were snoozing by the pile of puppies, raised their heads with ears on the alert.

Hearing someone shout Jordan's name like that could mean only one thing. They had been a fan.

"You watched his webseries?" Fiona pulled her arms tight across her chest. It hurt, knowing that all she had to do was touch a button and she could pull up hours of her brilliant, witty husband making history fun with his quirky sense of humor and easy-to-understand explanations.

"A big fan. I loved how he always compared Henry VIII and his wives to a bad soap opera. I can't believe I didn't recognize you."

Fiona shrugged. "I'm not exactly famous. I was only on for a few episodes."

"No, no, he always had your picture over his red 'Chair of Big Thoughts,'" Blake explained, face animated in a way that Fiona hadn't seen before. "There was a segment he used to do. It was something like—"

"'Things My Wife Knows That I Don't.'" Fiona laughed. "I'm flattered that you remembered."

"So, why is some big shot—"

"Small-time," Fiona corrected swiftly, one hand cutting off his words as if slicing through the air. "He was big-time. I wasn't. I mean, I'm not. I'm a little professor and a little researcher. I used to be bigger. My career and my hobbies used to matter more, mean more. When I look around here..." Fiona's gaze went pointedly to the kennels, then to the overgrown garden, "I think your life used to be fuller. Maybe full in a different way. If you're about to ask me why I want to help, it's just because I want to. I can relate. And yes, I'm looking for things to distract me from the holes I can't seem to fill."

There. I was honest. I was vulnerable. If he doesn't want my help, I walk away.

Blake followed her gaze. "The dogs were Peggy's passion. They take a lot of time, care, and grooming. Showing them was her hobby. I always treated them more like pets instead of investments."

"They *are* valuable. What do you charge per puppy?"

Blake cocked his head and a slow smile spread across his face. "You check out, but I can't let you help me for free."

Stupid male pride, Fiona thought. "I don't want your money. I told you, I can work from anywhere. I won't be losing anything but lonely hours in an empty house." *Wow. Pathetic much?*

"Would you take the pick of the litter in exchange for your troubles? It's not payment, per se, more like bartering."

Fiona had to stop herself from jumping and squealing. Instead, she rocked forward on her toes and dug her fingers into her arms where they rested across her chest. "Yes! The little one with the dark gray coat. Please."

"He's all yours." Blake stuck out his hand.

Fiona took it and shook it, trying not to show her shock at how her emotions surged. It had been a long time since a strong, masculine hand had enveloped hers and made her feel like she was a partner again. Even though it was only a partner in solving a mystery, not a life partner.

All of her senses still went on high alert and it irritated her.

As Fiona and Blake compared schedules, she forced down any tiny stirrings of interest in the man beside her.

Strictly business. Keeping Hannah safe and your mind occupied is the goal.

That's it.

That's all.

"Come on, Mac."

Fiona drove away, feeling guilty.

Macbeth put his paws up on the passenger's side window and whimpered.

"You liked it there, didn't you, boy? Did you like being with Biscuit and those puppies? Don't worry, we'll visit soon."

But a nagging little voice warned Fiona that visiting might not be enough. It might simply make her yearning for a family of her own worse.

Chapter Eight

Fiona brought her copy of the police report with her when she returned to Blake's home the following day and greeted him with a cheery, "I brought Macbeth, I hope that's okay. Here's the police report. I let the officer know that it was a black truck with a hanging bumper. It had a reflective sticker with some writing on it. Also, pound cake?"

Blake watched her pass, a faintly bewildered look on his face and sawdust in his hair, which was sticking up at odd angles around a pair of safety goggles. "Uh. He had a sports car. A Miata. It's black, but that's where the similarities end. Like I said, he might not be doing the dirty work himself. Anyone could have gotten into the outdoor kennel. That's why I keep all the dogs on the porch at night now and only let them play outside when I'm watching."

"If you're watching, you can't be working, right?"

Blake nodded, looking defeated, shoulders suddenly hanging. "I wonder if that's part of his game? Making me so overwhelmed that I can't protect Hannah, the animals, the property, *and* work. The state pays for Hannah's care now, but next month that will end. If my bank balance takes a big hit—" Blake stopped speaking, his mouth snapping shut. "Pound cake sounds good."

Fiona nodded. "What are you working on now?"

"A big order for the Glencastle Country Club. They have a private reception hall called the Oak Room for weddings and fancy parties. They want twelve hand-crafted, hand-carved chairs with scrollwork and cut-outs for their head table. Two of them are 'thrones.'"

"Yeesh." Fiona shook her head. "Oh, well. I guess the bride and groom can do what they want. It's their special day and it only comes around once."

Yep. Only once.

No second chances for the real thing, right? No one could ever replace Jordan. I could try to fill the holes, but no one else will ever fit.

Blake got out at three heavily glazed clayware plates, probably crafted by Peggy. As he sliced the thick, golden pound cake, he shared, "Peggy and I got married in our backyard. Not this one, but the smaller homestead we had. It was an acre and a half, but that was enough to start with. Everyone sat on picnic blankets."

Hm. Fiona nodded. Something odd was happening. Her heart, which usually recoiled in pain when she had to talk about Jordan or the intimate moments of their lives, suddenly wanted to join in. "Jordan and I got married at the historical society in my hometown. They rent it out. Beautiful place for photos—not so great for the other amenities. Can you imagine telling your guests not to touch anything on the walls or sit on the furniture? Jordan's cousin was the official 'Don't touch that!' guy for the day. But we loved it."

"That's not so bad. My mother-in-law got ants in her dress and knocked over the dessert table."

"Oh no! The cake?"

"Already cut, thank goodness."

"And speaking of cake—would Hannah like some? I see you have three plates."

"Hannah-Banana! Miss Fiona, Macbeth, and yummy cake are here!"

"Yummycake! Yummycake! What's yummycake?" Hannah came barreling out of a room to the south of the kitchen, her hands gray and slimy.

"It's something you can't eat with those muddy paws, little clay monster." Blake grabbed the toddler and hoisted her up on his hip so she could put her hands under the sink's faucet.

"Hi, Miss Fiona! Macbeth! Biscuit, your sweetheart is here!" Hannah struggled down and promptly picked up Macbeth. "I'll take you to your puppies."

Blake didn't meet her eyes as he sat down three plates at the table. "Um. Did I mention she's stubborn?"

"All us redheads are," Fiona tossed her hair, currently in a long braid, back with a smug grin. "I don't think Macbeth minds."

Fiona didn't feel the need to divulge that Mcbeth had been restless and sniffing for the puppies all evening. Nor did she mention that he'd been whimpering and whining most of the morning, making it a struggle to teach classes without feeling like she had to go check on him.

"You know how kids are. Hannah's got three adult dogs and five puppies, but what does she want? The one she doesn't have."

"I know what that's like. So blessed, but sometimes I still want what I don't have." *A baby. Jordan to come back. A family of my own to live with and raise.*

Focus, Fiona. "Did you say Reyes works at a carwash?"

"Yes, but I don't think that's where the bulk of his money comes from."

"But maybe it's where he and his friends hang out? I'll drive by there on my way home and see if I spot a black pick up. Then I can drive past his house and see if it's around. It could be a car he borrowed but doesn't own."

"Just be careful. I don't want him hassling you." Blake put down a pitcher of water with mint leaves in it, banging it down so that water splashed over the top.

Fiona nodded. "I'll be careful. He sounds like a rough character, to put it mildly.

Blake sat across from her. "Do you need to work? I mean, teach a virtual class?"

"No, I just have essays to read today. I can do that while I play with Hannah and the puppies."

"She hasn't napped yet, so she may konk out soon. If that happens, I have the box of Olivia's belongings."

"Olivia?"

"Hannah's mother."

"Oh, right. Yes. Did you look through them and see if anyone named Tyler was mentioned?"

Blake closed his eyes as if he was in pain, the fork with fluffy yellow cake falling back to his plate. "I tried. I opened it up in the guest room, and then—I fell asleep. I know. I'm terrible. I have those chairs to finish by the end of May, and laundry to fold, and Hannah's still waking up once a night to use the potty... Parenting alone is hard. But it's worth it! I'm not complaining. Or looking to trade it for anything."

"Blake, I get it. Well, no I can't *understand*, but I can imagine. I wish I was in your shoes, more than you know. Do you have any relatives who can help out?"

He nodded slowly. "My mother isn't nearby, but she intends to come out during the summer. Peggy's parents are closer, but they're having a hard time with the idea of fostering. They're afraid to lose a grandchild."

Guilt stabbed Fiona. That was one reason she hadn't pursued foster care. She had worried about a child being taken away, or a child refusing to bond with her.

I'm a selfish piece of scum, aren't I?

"H-how do you deal with it? Knowing that you could lose her. I mean, what if we find this Tyler guy, and—" Fiona shuffled the cake around her plate, none of it making its way to her mouth.

"I thought I'd have Peggy forever, too. God doesn't promise us a person on this earth forever. Forever can have different addresses."

Blake shrugged, looking at his plate. "Figure I can have Hannah for a little while or a long time. Wouldn't be up to me, anyway."

"You're very wise."

A heavy, tarry weight in Fiona's chest lifted slightly, and then seemed to break free and float off as she heard Hannah's giggling shriek.

"If Hannah naps, I could go through Olivia's papers?" Fiona offered.

Blake nodded. "Just one problem."

"What's that?"

"Who writes things down anymore? We'd need Olivia's phone or her laptop—and that's something we don't have."

Fiona sipped her refreshing, minty water, watching the green leaves with their wrinkled surfaces swirling against the ice cubes. "What was her last name?"

"Thompson."

"Did you ever search her accounts and find—" Fiona stopped talking as Blake shook his head emphatically.

"The only accounts I have are business-related. I have the website and it has social media integrations. I make a few posts a week with pictures of the puppies or our furniture in progress and the website sends them out and links them to the social feeds." He held up his hands and then brushed them back through his hair, pushing the curling bits of wood from the wavy tangles. "As you can tell, I work more with my hands than screens."

Fiona grinned and patted the wide leather satchel she carried, which now rested on the floor at her feet. "I'm the opposite. If she had any accounts that weren't private or closed after her death, I can at least see old posts and photographs. Maybe we'll get lucky and find something."

The carpenter snorted. "If we find something, it won't be luck. It'll be a miracle."

Fiona grinned. "I think God is on Hannah's side."

FIONA SAT ON THE SUNNY porch with an overflowing cardboard box at her feet. Macbeth and Biscuit were once again napping. The puppies were nursing contentedly as the adult dogs rested nose-to-nose. Hannah was asleep on a little cot set in the corner, hair fluttering over her cheek every time she took a deep, sighing breath. In the distance, she could hear Wharton and Wilma (the Westies) playing in the big outdoor kennel, their occasional barks a sharp note in the steady chorus of Blake's scroll saw.

It was nice.

She and Jordan used to spend days working together. They had their desks in the same office, or they put their laptops on their knees and sat side by side on the sofa. When they were working on a joint area of research, their kitchen table was a free-for-all of papers and sticky notes. That was the dream. That level of togetherness and shared purpose.

It was funny how peaceful she felt, just hearing Blake working away while she finished posting her grades for the week and turned her attention to the box in front of her.

Olivia Thompson... Who were you?

A college athlete.

Pictures revealed the dark-haired woman in a dozen diving poses.

Medals. Ribbons.

High school yearbooks.

Baby pictures of Hannah.

Lots of pamphlets and affirmations from various rehab centers, creased, croupled, and tear stained.

A cellphone with a shattered screen.

Jewelry, the affordable costume kind from the mall.

A name tag, the kind servers at restaurants wear.

Empty orange bottles from various pharmacies, each one with a different painkiller's name on the label.

Everything of value was gone, but yet everything in the box had immense value, telling a story without a single word.

"Oh, Olivia." Fiona traced a picture with a gentle fingertip. "You didn't mean to leave her. I—" Fiona's whisper stopped abruptly. The photographs were sticking together, humidity of long storage impacting them. Fiona decided she'd put together a nice photo album for Hannah—but first she had to pry the photos apart. That's when the chain fell out.

It was a gold chain with a golden charm dangling from it. A charm in the shape of a T.

"Of course. T for Thompson."
But something didn't sit right.
Fiona began laying the photos out on the floor at her feet.
Olivia often had a necklace on, even in the photos where she was diving.
It was always the same necklace—a silver cross.

Fiona squinted at all the photos available. In every photo, Olivia wore small stud earrings or no earrings and the cross necklace. All of her jewelry was silver, which complimented her flawless skin and her bright blue eyes.

"She never wears yellow gold. And this is a man's necklace. I *think* this is a man's necklace."

"Came to check on you."

Fiona yelped and jumped, trying not to land on any of the pictures. She'd been so caught up in examining the photos that she hadn't noticed the noise of the saw had ceased. "Is this a man's necklace?"

Blake looked at the chain. "I think it looks like a more masculine cut, yeah. But I'm no expert. I only ever wore one piece of jewelry." He waggled his bare hand, now ringless.

"Well, this is a T."

Blake gave her a look. "I'm a carpenter, not an illiterate."

Fiona rolled her eyes. "This is a very masculine style for a girl who always seemed to dress in a feminine style. It's dark yellow gold, and she always wore silver jewelry. Also..." Fiona hefted the chain in her hand and tested its weight. She turned it over and looked for the hallmark. "It's heavy. The charm is 14 karat gold. That doesn't add up."

Blake raised his eyebrows, and his shoulders followed. "Why not? It could have been a gift from someone who didn't know her style. Her last name was Thompson. Lots of people wear monogram jewelry."

"One, this is a gold necklace, real gold, and it's heavy. It's a good piece of jewelry, but it wasn't in the bag of costume jewelry, it was matted in between these pictures. Olivia's belongings don't have much monetary value. Why?"

"My guess would be because she was a struggling single mother addicted to narcotics."

"Exactly. She probably sold or traded valuable pieces. She kept this one. Why?"

"It could have been her father's?"

Fiona's mouth froze, hanging open. "Oh." So much for the breakthrough.

Blake took the chain from her hand and squinted at it. "I think this is pretty new, though. The design and the style remind me of things I've seen the younger guys wear."

"So what if this isn't her necklace? What if it's Tyler's, the sweetheart's? She kept it because it meant a lot to her, so much that she couldn't even sell it.'

Blake looked into the box. "There wasn't much left of value."

Fiona waited, expecting to have her idea dismissed as too fantastical.

Instead, Blake grabbed the high school yearbook. "Maybe a high school sweetheart? Let's see if we can find anyone named Tyler in here."

"I can do that. You have to work."

Blake shook his head. "I was able to get a lot done today—for the first time since Hannah came to stay with me. It was the first time someone was watching her. Even when she naps, I work slower. I'm always listening to see if Hannah is awake or getting into mischief." Blake cleared his throat and flipped the pages. "Thanks, Fiona. That's what I wanted to say."

Fiona nodded and said nothing as she bent to gather the photographs and placed them in neat stacks.

It was a companionable quiet that resonated in her mind, and she liked it.

"STAY FOR SUPPER?" BLAKE asked after forty minutes of dutifully poring over every page in Olivia's yearbook and coming up with a dozen possibilities—but none of them seemed likely.

"Oh, I couldn't."

"Stay."

Hannah was up, rubbing her eyes and stumbling off her cot.

"Hey, Hannah-Banana. Bathroom break and then it's time to help feed the chickens and the puppies." Blake switched from investigator and carpenter to a warm, friendly father in a split-second.

"I'll stay for supper if I can help make it," Fiona called as Blake led Hannah to the downstairs half bathroom.

"It's a deal. The chili is already in the slow cooker. How are you at cornbread?"

"Uhh. Got a recipe?" Fiona followed them out to the kitchen.

BLAKE WENT OUT TO DO chores. Hannah sat up on the kitchen island, a bowl balanced in her lap as she stirred vigorously. Fiona was covered in as much cornmeal and flour as was in the bowl, but she was laughing as hard as Hannah. Macbeth and the puppy parade were in the kitchen now, too, squirming and wriggling, looking to be near the center of the excitement.

"This is fun. Funner with you." Hannah leaned forward without warning and planted her wet hand on Fiona's shirt, balling the fabric up in her little first as she gave a happy grin.

Fiona squealed and caught the mixture as it was about to careen out of the little girl's lap. "This is fun. Funner with you, too." She leaned forward and planted a kiss on top of her strawberry curls.

"Make it again?"

"Cornbread? I'm sure we'll make it again. Okay, what's left in the bowl is mixed as possible. Ready to pour it in the pan with me?"

Hannah tipped the bowl. The whole thing fell from her slippery grasp with a plop. "That's okay," Fiona reassured, lifting it out and shaking it.

"Make it again?" Hannah demanded, wriggling as she tried to get down.

"Yep, I want to make it again."

"Now?"

"Oh, no. Not now. We have to eat this first."

"Tomorrow."

"I won't be here tomorrow, I..." Fiona stopped. Tomorrow was the weekend. What would she be doing that was so urgent? Spending time with her chickens and posting the week's assignments? Walking for hours over the same trail, misery eating her alive?

"Maybe you can come visit me sometime. I don't have toys, but I have a big yard and big playpen where you can climb in with the puppies."

"I can bring toys!" Hannah clambered down, using the toddler step stool next to the cabinets.

"Uh. Wait! We have to ask Daddy."

"Ask me what?" Blake came in, toeing off his work boots and heading to the sink.

"If you and Hannah would like to have lunch at my house tomorrow," Fiona decided quickly.

"Oh." Blake looked surprised.

To be honest, she was surprised, too.

What am I doing? I don't need to have them over. I don't need to get attached to this little girl.

Or the guy.

"We could drive past the carwash Reyes works at and scope out the cars." *No. No, tell me I didn't just say scope out. That makes me sound like I'm trying to be cool—and failing.*

Blake faltered at the sink, knocking the soap dispenser into it, grabbing it back, and accidentally turning on the attached sprayer. It splashed down into the soaking mixing bowl and ricocheted a fountain back onto his chest.

"I withdraw the offer. Sorry, I didn't mean to make—"

"I'd love to! No, I really would. When Hannah came to stay, we went to the park and the zoo, the mall, the ice cream shop, story hour, Music and Me classes... All of those fun places. When Reyes came sniffing around, I started staying close to home. I felt like I didn't have someone to watch my back and I..." Blake dropped his voice as he mopped up his shirt, "I didn't want to tell anyone what was going on. I was afraid they'd take her away." He sighed as he unbuttoned the wet plaid shirt he wore over his gray t-shirt. "Stupid, huh? Selfish?"

Fiona forced herself to do something useful. As she looked in the cupboards for bowls, she replied, "More like scared. I've only known Hannah for a couple of days, and I would hate to lose her!"

"Where I going?" Hannah's voice demanded, higher than usual.

Blake dropped his shirt to the counter and scooped up his foster daughter. "To Miss Fiona's house for a picnic lunch? And a Saturday afternoon drive? Is that fun, Hannah Bunny?"

Hannah squealed as Blake bounced her on his hip.

Fiona bit her lip as she put the bowls next to the slow cooker and grabbed a ladle for the chili. No, she didn't want to lose this, and she didn't want Hannah to lose another parent.

The bowls were perfect, smooth, and glazed in shades of blue. The bottom of each bowl had a little spray of flowers with a P in the middle.

Peggy Wells.

Fiona took the reminders that Peggy Wells had left her mark on everything in the house, especially the man in it, and that was how it was supposed to stay.

Chapter Nine

Hannah, Macbeth, and Biscuit were running around the outside of the chicken coop. The puppies were playing inside the big puppy enclosure. Hannah was blowing bubbles, and the two older dogs were merrily chasing them.

"She really loves you. Loves it here." Blake closed his eyes and sighed.

Fiona sighed, too, sinking back in the Adirondack chair she'd pulled close to the puppy playpen. It was tempting to stay like this—mainly for Blake's sake. When he relaxed, his face looked calm and peaceful.

When he saw her computer screen, his face would change. "Blake?"

"Hm?"

"We promised Hannah we'd go get ice cream. There's a shop near the car wash. It'd be a good excuse to drive past."

Blake's face turned tense again. "Yep.'

"Although, he may not work on Saturdays."

"Nope."

Fiona rolled her eyes. Jordan was always so full of life, so full of words.

Jordan didn't have to worry about his little girl being taken away in three weeks.

"I was able to find some photos of Olivia on Instagram. I... I wanted to double check something. The man you're talking about, Reyes. Do you know his first name?"

"Hector."

"Do you know his nickname?"

Blake opened one eye. "Funny enough, we're not on a nickname basis."

"It's on his police record. Hector Reyes, alias Tank Reyes."

"Ha. Must be like when you call the biggest bruiser on the team 'Tiny.' Hector Reyes is a skinny little rip."

Fiona shoved her laptop into Blake's hands as they rested on his knees. "Look at these photos. They're all from a party that happened after Olivia was put on the injured list for the swim season a few years ago. See? 'Two more months until I can get back in the pool—I'll have a Blue Hawaiian instead.'"

"So she had a drink while she was underage. A lot of people make mistakes at parties in college. She— " Blake stopped speaking as his eyes focused on the picture.

Olivia was with a small crowd of people at a party.

The man standing behind her was Hector Reyes.

"Hector 'Tank' Reyes. T for Tyler? Or T for Tank?" Fiona asked softly, thinking of the gold chain and the charm they'd found.

"No. No, no man who knows he's the father would call his little girl the wrong name! Or threaten the man taking care of her! What if I were the same kind of scum he is and I retaliated?" Blake demanded, rising and pushing the computer back into her lap.

Fiona didn't answer. Olivia had either gotten a new profile or stopped updating this one shortly after Hannah was born. The last photo was of an infant with startling red curls in a pink onesie covered in strawberries. Scrolling back through the other pictures, all of which were visible to the public, Fiona felt her dread lessen. "He's only in the one photo that I can see. It could be a coincidence, just two strangers at a party."

"He'd have to be more than a stranger to know about her kid, wouldn't he?" Blake continued to pace. Biscuit and Macbeth seemed to think it was a game and followed him, chasing the trailing laces of his boots.

Fiona squinted. Hector Reyes was fond of gold jewelry, too. She didn't mention that to Blake. He looked like he was coming apart.

I wish I could help hold him together...

Fiona joined the dogs. "I mentioned the possibility because I'm a researcher and a historian. I get all the facts."

"Well, I'm a father. I don't want all the facts, I just want the facts that will keep Hannah safe—with me." Blake pushed his hair back. The thick locks sprang right back, curly and tousled across his forehead.

"Did you call your case worker back?" Fiona asked. "Have they heard anything new about a challenge to your adoption proceedings?"

"They don't work on the weekends. Last I heard, they hadn't received anything." Blake snorted. "That doesn't make me feel any better. It took them three months to put the original petition for adoption in their system. I hand delivered it to their office. It took three months to make it from a physical desk to some electronic letters on the screen! Dang it!" Blake kicked a stick out of the path and Macbeth went bounding after it.

He whirled abruptly and smacked into Fiona, broad chest to her narrow one, almost knocking her on her denim-covered bottom. He snagged her arms, pulling her back upright.

"Sorry!" they both exclaimed in unison.

"I didn't realize you were—"

"I wish I could—" Fiona trailed off. "I wish I could help."

Blake's hands kneaded on her elbows, his chin tucking down to look into her eyes. "You are the first person I've allowed to help me since Peggy passed away. People told me I was foolish to try to adopt alone. I got mad. I shut most people out. And then with this situation... I didn't know who to trust. Or *how* to trust people again." Blake's hands dropped. "Peggy was my best friend. My everything. My life partner and work partner, too."

When he pulled back, Fiona didn't let him retreat, nor did she retreat herself. She was nodding, eyes wide and bright, "Yes! Yes, exactly! Jordan was that for me, too. I get it. More than you know."

I get why we can help Hannah together, and that is all we can do together. If I ever thought, or even dreamt for a second, that Blake and I could move on from our past lives—it would be a mistake. No one can replace something like that, and we've both lived it. We know the truth.

Or maybe... Maybe only someone who knows exactly what it's like to lose perfection can take a gamble on something that seems so perfect, made out of broken pieces.

The spring air seemed to still as Fiona stood, looking up at him as thoughts whirred around her brain.

She had to put a stop to them. "Let's get that ice cream!

"THAT'S HIS CAR." BLAKE sat in the passenger seat up front while Hannah dozed in the high back booster that Blake had transferred from his truck.

"Reyes's car? Where?" Fiona cruised slowly down the main street of Glencastle's small retail and restaurant district. On a Saturday afternoon, it was bustling. Cars were lined up around the block to go to the car wash on the corner, desperate to get the last of the salt and slush off of their cars after a late-March blizzard.

"That little black convertible."

"But no black truck."

"This is a waste. Let's get the ice cream. My treat."

"Okay, we will. But first..." Fiona swerved out of the thoroughfare and into a spot a block away from the car wash. "Why don't I pick up the ice cream while Hannah naps?"

"Uh. Yeah, but she'll be miserable if we don't let her wake up and get a cone," Blake protested.

"We'll wake her up in a minute." Fiona slid out of the car and leaned down to meet Blake's confused gaze. "I'm going to go into the car wash first."

She left the keys in the ignition, shut the driver's door, and walked off, trying to keep her steps casual, and ignoring Blake's puzzled shout of "What?? But-but you're not *in* a car!"

FIONA LOOKED AT THE attendant who was sitting outside the entrance to the car wash tunnel. He had his eyes glued to his phone and he mindlessly pushed the button that moved cars on without taking his eyes from the screen. She'd seen Reyes before, and this wasn't him.

Fiona looked at the boxy gray building next to the car wash. Through the window, she could see racks of chamois, hard wax, and car-specific cleaners. A sign on the door advertised detailing packages and buy-one-get-one-free squeegees.

If Reyes' car is here, he must be here. He's not the guy drying the wet cars as they come out. He's not the guy letting them in. He must be in the office. Fiona took a deep breath and pushed open the creaking door, trying to look interested in the racks of supplies.

No one was in the shop.

Defeat slumped her shoulders. *What are you doing, playing detective, you idiot? Go back to Hannah and Blake!*

"No! I told you I'll have it soon. I don't have it now. I need something he wants, first. He's inside, man. It *has* to be her. What else is he gonna care about? Nah, I'll let you know after I see him. I'll drive up once it's worth it."

Fiona picked up a neon spray bottle of Meguiar's Ceramic Detailer and pretended to study it. Her arms developed goosebumps despite the muggy interior of the building. Reyes had just entered from a backroom and was now standing behind her, talking on his phone.

"Gotta go. Lunch is over. Later this week." Reyes ended his call and addressed her in a brusque voice. "You need something?"

"I...I'm trying to find a product." *Brilliant reply, Fiona.*

"Like what?" Reyes came over beside her, dark eyes impatient.

Fiona turned to face him. This man had *no* resemblance to Hannah, not even a miniscule amount. He had a proud, straight nose, dark pecan skin, and coffee-colored eyes that gave an unfriendly warning. Why? He doesn't know who I am. Does he not like that I'm in here, interrupting something else he could be doing?

"I—I want the safest cleaning products possible. I'm not always in town and I thought I'd get some supplies to keep in my garage. I have a dog and a toddler at home." Fiona took out her phone. "I also have a terrible memory. Can you tell me what products are safest and I'll take pictures? I like to get the same brands each time once I know what to get."

Reyes looked startled. "Uh. None of these would be safe if your kid or dog ate 'em. They're not for consumption, right?"

"Right. But some must be safer than others?" Fiona pressed, opening her camera app.

"I guess these. These are all good." Reyes gestured vaguely to the right side of the wall and turned back to the desk.

Fiona picked up a jug of soap and held it out from her body. Her phone was angled to have Reyes in the shot. "Great, thanks." She hit the "Record" button on the video function of her phone instead of taking a still shot. Please let his hunch pay off, she prayed silently. "You know how careful you have to be with toddlers. They're into everything. Do you have kids?"

"Nope. Don't have a dog, either." Reyes sank back onto a stool behind the register, eyes on his phone.

"Mhm. Oh, I left my wallet in the car. Be back in a minute." Heart pounding, Fiona left the shop.

BLAKE WAS PACING OUTSIDE the car, Hannah asleep on his shoulder. "What the heck? Where were you?" he demanded in a stage whisper.

"I told you, I went to the car wash."

"Without a car! What if Reyes had realized you were with us? He... he could have done something. That guy is sick if he kidnaps puppies, or tells someone else to kidnap puppies!" Blake's eyes sparked.

In answer Fiona pulled out her phone and pressed play.

"You went to buy turtle wax?" Blake looked at her as if trying to see where she'd hidden it.

"Shh. Listen."

"That's him!" Blake pointed to the phone, his hand then going protectively to cradle Hannah's drowsy head.

"I know! Listen," Fiona repeated, putting the phone low between their bodies, her eyes scanning the quietly bustling streets. She heard own voice coming out through the speaker. "You know how careful you have to be with toddlers. They're into everything. Do you have kids?"

"Nope. Don't have a dog, either."

Blake's head jerked up. "We got him."

Chapter Ten

"We don't got him... except in our own minds."

Fiona stopped scrambling her Sunday morning eggs to push the phone further under her chin. She had celebrated with Hannah and Blake last night, taking ice cream cones to the park and feeding the ducks. Then, they ended up visiting the Wells' place, where all nine dogs were in a terrier tornado, playing tug-of-war and chasing balls that Hannah threw for them.

It had been idyllic—and for the first time in three years, Fiona hadn't felt sad looking at someone else's baby, hadn't felt lonely hearing a man's laughter.

But Blake wasn't laughing now.

"What do you mean?" Fiona pressed, tipping half the eggs into Macbeth's bowl at her feet and half onto a plate for herself.

"I'm pretty sure that your recording of him isn't legal evidence."

"Sometimes courts make exceptions when the welfare of a child is at stake. How would the court think Reyes is a better choice for Hannah? He has a criminal record and a history of substance abuse? Blake, even if this goes to court, they probably wouldn't let Hannah go to him."

"But if he's the father, that doesn't matter. Blood trumps."

"No, *heart* triumphs. There's probably at least enough evidence to make the judge doubt his claim that he's the biological father. The judge would order a DNA test."

Blake's voice was a protective snarl, "And how long does it take? Everything takes longer in the system. I don't know what they'd do with Hannah in the meantime. And then once the results come back?"

"Even if Reyes was the father, there's no evidence that he'd be a good one or a safe one. In fact," Fiona put her fork down with a thoughtful frown, "he sounded like he was still mixed up in some shady business when I was at the car wash. I heard him on the phone. He was telling someone on the phone about getting a package for someone else. Someone 'inside.'"

Blake's voice was muffled by whimpering and yapping. "Hold on. Hannah, put one yellow scoop in the Biscuit's bowl. Good job! You're the best helper."

Fiona smiled and pictured the little girl, probably in cute pajamas, taking care of the little Cairn terrier litter and their mama.

"Someone inside where?" Blake asked when he returned to the conversation.

"I'm not big on my slang and streetsmarts, but isn't that pretty universal for someone who's in prison? Going away? Doing time? On the inside?"

Blake's voice was absent for a long moment. Fiona looked at the phone screen to make sure they hadn't been disconnected. "That jerk wants my little girl for some criminal in prison? What— What in the—" Blake broke off into angry spluttering.

"Daddy? Are you mad?"

"Yes, pumpkin. Why don't you go get your sippy cup and—"

"You could get Fiona. She'll make it better."

Fiona put a hand to her mouth, and then to her heart. *Oh my goodness. Sweet little peanut.* "Blake, if the guy is on the inside, as in prison, there is no way that Hannah would be in danger from him. Whatever nightmare is in your mind, let it go."

"Fiona, you're not a parent. I can't just 'let it go.'"

As suddenly as her happy thoughts had bloomed, Fiona's sense of emptiness returned, drowning them. "No. I'm not. But I still had an idea."

Blake's voice was soft and contrite. "I'm an idiot. Forgive me?"

"Sure."

"If you and Macbeth come over after church, we could collect honey and put some burgers on the grill. First cook-out of the season?"

Happiness struggled—but it rose. The heart is made to rise again, Fiona thought to herself. "Wait—did you say collect honey?"

"From our hives."

Fiona winced. "Sounds fun. And I can tell you what I want to research next."

"I'm not a patient person. Give me a hint."

Fiona chuckled. "One, you must be a patient person—you raise animals and garden. You make things with your hands."

"Get to two quickly. See? The patience is a limited edition thing."

She could envision the sparkle in his eye as he spoke. Fiona smiled to herself. She liked the way Blake smiled. The way he laughed.

Get a grip!

"Okay, here's an idea. Reyes is claiming to be Hannah's father. He must be really certain that no one else will come forward to challenge that, but not sure enough to pursue it legally. We know he wants to get something for someone 'on the inside.' What if Hannah's father is in jail? What if Reyes wants to use her as some kind of leverage over him?"

Blake picked up the thread of her story. "It'd have to be a man who would want to know about his daughter. It would have to be someone who might not realize what's going on, or even that Olivia passed away. It's likely that it's someone local, too. Reyes' record is all state and local. Olivia was local."

Excitement swelled in her chest and ran down to her calves. She started rocking from foot to foot, finally giving in and running up the stairs to get dressed. "So we look at local arrests made in the last three years, and we look for people who were associates of Reyes or Olivia's."

"And we especially look for someone named Tyler. Or who has the initial T. Reyes is scum; I refuse to believe Olivia would have anything to do with him."

"Sadly, drugs do change people," Fiona mourned. "For Reyes to know this much about Hannah—faulty as his information is—I'm wondering if he wasn't one of Olivia's suppliers at some point. She may have told him who the father was. Or maybe the father is the connection between Reyes and Olivia. We don't know what kind of man he is, either. Except that he's probably in prison." Fiona felt gloom settle over her.

Blake's voice chased it away. "We're going to make sure Hannah's always safe and loved. That's what Olivia would have wanted. And... no. Sorry. I better let you go."

"What is it? What were you going to say?" Fiona demanded, heart thudding.

"You'll think I'm crazy."

The thudding increased. Fiona pushed on her chest as if she could stop the hummingbird inside from zipping around so much. Blake wasn't going to say anything worthy of a racing heart. Did she even want such a thing?

Shut up and listen, Fiona! He hasn't said anything yet!

"This is fun. Having you help us. Having you around. I know the situation is serious, but...you've made a bad patch a better one. Thanks, Fiona."

"You're welcome. It's been good for me, too."

Macbeth let out a loud yap from the doorway. "Oh. Macbeth says hi."

"Hey, Mac. Your girl is missing you," Blake called, and Fiona could hear the smile in his voice.

"His girl, huh? Is Biscuit his girl?"

"Well, she'd like to be. I can tell. Macbeth's a stand-up pup, willing to help protect her kids and taking care of them when things were bad… He takes after his owner. Th-that's the kind of person, I mean, dog, that I would—that Biscuit would look for after losing her mate and having kids to raise on her own. What do you think?"

The hummingbird in her chest was back, and it had lost control, swooping and dipping along with her stomach. "I think that sounds about right. I'll be over later."

Fiona hung up and flopped over backward on her bed. It had barely been a week. There was no way she could be falling for this guy.

"He was just talking about the dogs, right?"

Macbeth took a running leap and cleared the bed, coming over to sniff her and nuzzle her cheek. "Looks like you've got a family in the works, little man. Now, how do I fit in?"

Chapter Eleven

How could the most stressful situation make her so happy?

The last week of April was sunny and warm. Each day, Fiona taught her classes on campus and then rushed out to Blake's, where she was supposed to be combing through public files of arrests and court hearings, looking for a Tyler from this area.

Her searches were regularly interrupted by Hannah demanding to sit on her lap and read, cuddle next to her in a pile of puppies as they watched a cartoon, or go into the kitchen and make muffins, cupcakes, or cornbread.

Macbeth was in doggie heaven. The wobbly puppies were now sure on their feet and he was the referee to endless disputes, nipping gently when one of the five got too rambunctious, and napping nose-to-nose with his sweetheart.

Blake Wells looked like a different person than the sullen, wary man who'd come to the door. In just two weeks, he'd gone from permanently worried and angry to someone who made her laugh and who impressed her with his skills around the house and homestead.

The last day of April, a sunny Sunday turned into a wet downpour, bending the heads of tulips to the ground and causing all nine of the dogs to growl at the sky from where they watched the storm on the enclosed porch.

"I made you something. Hannah helped." Blake tossed the statement out along with a small wooden box, an intricate thing of lattice work and curlicues.

Fiona looked away from her laptop and pulled the box across the tables. "This is beautiful. You *made* this?"

"Mhm." Blake lifted the lid and showed Fiona a folded drawing stuffed inside. "That's Hannah's contribution. It's a thank you from both of us. We really appreciate you."

"Aww, Blake. I—I got a ping! I got a ping!" Fiona temporarily forgot the box as her computer screen changed from a line of scrolling text to a solid white box with the words "Search Criteria Found One Record."

Blake crashed into one of his beautiful hand-carved chairs and dragged it around so both of them were eyeballing the screen. "This looks much more legit than the program I was using."

"The university history department has access to the public records department, and in Pennsylvania, criminal records are a matter of public record, even though the school can't use them to screen educational candidates. We mainly use it for the older records, going back to Glencastle's creation in the late 1700s. Land deeds, county disputes, that sort of thing," Fiona rambled, fingers flying.

"But there have to be hundreds of Tylers in three hundred years," Blake squinted at the screen.

"Not hundreds of Tylers in just three years, though. He would have had to be out of prison around three-and-a-half years ago in order to meet Olivia and form a relationship with her. He could be anywhere in the world, of course, but Reyes said he'd drive to see this person." Fiona pushed doubt away. *Fell into place too easily. I shouldn't have heard that call. It was a freak coincidence.*

Nothing has been easy about what Blake and Hannah are going through. Nothing is easy about what I went through. Adoption is hard. Widowhood is hard.

God is good. God doesn't do coincidences. He guides steps.

"If he's going to drive, he has to be local. And if it were a big crime, he wouldn't be just waltzing in. He'd be in some maximum security facility. Oh, my gosh. My gosh—" Blake seized her hand, squeezing it hard. "What if he wants Hannah? He could want Hannah, this stranger in a cell who hasn't even met her. What if he's worse than Reyes. Stop." Blake grabbed both her hands before she could open the PDF of the file.

Fiona didn't know what to say. She laced her fingers gently through his. "It's okay to be scared. God wouldn't do this without a reason."

Blake laughed, a wet bitter sound. "What reason could he have to take Peggy and Jordan? To make drugs and get people addicted to them?"

"Daddy, I need—" Hannah waddled in. Her eyes went wide and she pointed a chubby finger at their clasped hands. "Sweethearts!"

Fiona pulled her hands back guiltily as if she'd been burned.

Blake didn't, slowly reclaiming her hand across the table. "Sweet friends, my Hannah-banana. What did you need?"

"Need a snack." Hannah climbed up on her foster father's lap and put her head on his shoulder. "Cheesy crackers?"

"I'll get you some, sweetie."

Fiona waited until he rose. What reasons did God have for bad things?

She looked at the sweet little girl clinging to Blake as he carried her to the cabinets. Those little fingers digging into his shirt as she nuzzled her cheek in more deeply.

"Maybe you wouldn't have done certain things if Peggy were here. I wouldn't have been working at home if Jordan was around, if I hadn't been trying to keep my schedule free because of the adoption...that fell through. I don't know why God does certain things, but I trust Him on it."

"Me, too," Hannah piped up with a firm nod.

Blake and Fiona exchanged a look. It was likely the child had no idea what the meaning was behind those words, but her earnest conviction was adorable.

"Well, if you two ladies say so, I'd better agree. Hannah, want to help me run the extractor?"

"Fiona! The honey 'stractor!" Hannah kicked her feet in giddy excitement as Blake sat her on the counter. "It goes so fast! Spinning!"

"You and Daddy go run the extractor. I'm going to read through this file."

BLAKE CAME BACK, HERDING Hannah along with a small glass jar of honey clutched proudly in her arms.

"For you."

"You're sweeter than the honey, honey bunny," Fiona let Hannah climb into her lap.

Blake silently took the sheet of paper she'd been writing notes on.

Tyler Hanes

23 at time of arrest on possession of illegal substances and intent to sell. DUI. Breaking and entry. Sentenced to five years.

Known associates:

Hector "The Tank" Reyes

Kenny "King" Mitford

Olivia Thompson

Recent action: Petition for expedited parole hearing—May 5th. Status: Pending.

OLIVIA THOMPSON

DUI

Plea entered: Not guilty.

Medical waiver.

Fine for driving under the influence.

"ONE OF THE DATES ON Tyler Hanes' record matches the date of Olivia's—uh—incident. It was one of the early ones on his sheet. They both got fines."

"Did they meet there, you think?" Blake asked, voice neutral, his eyes saying more than he would voice in front of Hannah, even though her understanding was limited.

Fiona swirled the jar, watching Hannah's eyes follow the thick golden honey as it moved slowly. "I would guess before. It's not clear, but I'm wondering if they were both in the car when it was pulled over."

Blake nodded with a soft grunt, eyes still scanning the paper.

Fiona offered, "He's at the Carbon County Correctional Facility. An hour or two up the turnpike. We could go... *I* could go."

Blake came over and took Hannah in his arms. "There are some beautiful parks up that way, and I'm ahead of schedule with the chairs for the country club. The puppies aren't old enough to be left alone inside for half a day, yet, but I could ask my neighbor to check on them. We could make a half-day of it. Take turns watching Hannah?"

"I like when you're both together," Hannah said, grabbing Blake's stubbled cheeks and squishing his lean face until he had fishlips. "Silly Daddy."

"Silly princess. You go play while Miss Fiona and I work out some details."

Hannah hopped down and Fiona finally took a moment to look in the beautifully carved box. Her fingers caressed the paper as she opened it and saw a drawing of two pink blobs and five smaller brown blobs. "Wow! I love this, Hannah." *I have no idea what it is, but she made it for me and therefore, it's my favorite drawing ever.*

"Love you, too! It's the puppies and the mommy and daddy dog!" Hannah sang, hopping away.

Silence was left in her wake.

She loves me, too.

She's two. She doesn't grasp the concept of love.

Fiona's heart didn't believe that. Love is something you can't limit with brain cells and numbers.

"She's getting very attached to you," Blake murmured, tapping his fingers idly on the paper.

"I know. I can stay away for a while if you think it would be better for her—"

"I was thinking you ought to be around more. You know. For Hannah. That is, if you're interested."

Fiona nodded. "I'd love to see her every day, if our schedules mesh." Her cheeks felt warm and she kept her head turned away from the man addressing her. Looking for something to say, she settled on discussing the carved box. "Thank you again, Blake. This is incredibly intricate. I can't imagine how long it must take to make something like this." *Wait. It can't take that long. If it took so long, he wouldn't have given it to me. I'm just a friend. A helper.*

"Well... Six hours on that one, but I'd already put the box together. I make a lot of decorative boxes to sell in the shop or online."

See? Nothing special.

"But they're not usually done with that level of detail. This is one of my best, I gotta say." Blake came over, standing close behind her and turning the box in her palm to show her that every centimeter of every side was adorned with his workmanship.

"Blake! Six hours... it's amazing, but when did you have time?"

His chin brushed her temple before he took a quick step back. "Last night. Couldn't sleep."

"Thinking about the adoption and Reyes?" Fiona gave him a look of sympathy, praying her blush would die down. She must look like one of the red tulips by the porch.

"No. Other things."

Chapter Twelve

The drive to Carbon County Correctional Facility was surprisingly beautiful. Macbeth and Hannah sat in the back of Fiona's car while she drove. Blake offered to drive on the way back.

"It's not going to be a long trip. I'm glad they're letting us speak to him. They said I can use my phone and video call. That way we can both talk to him at once, but we won't have to bring Hannah inside." The tall man's hands flexed onto his knees, then fiddled with the window switch, then his hair, and back to his knees.

"You don't know what to do when your hands aren't busy. I don't know what to do when my brain isn't busy. Or my mouth. I talk a lot when I'm nervous."

"I fidget. I'd whittle, but it makes a mess on the upholstery."

"Ooh! I know what. Hold your hands," Hannah suggested from the back.

Fiona blinked. Blake looked out the window.

Suddenly, her hand shot out and grasped his. They both seemed to still.

Not Hannah. "No! Your own hand! Like this." The toddler held up her hands above her head and folded them. "Miss J. says, 'Hands can snap. Hands can clap. Hands together—" Hannah paused to smush her plump palms together and interlock her fingers, "and now I put them in my lap!"

"Miss J is the Sunday School teacher. Honey, Miss Fiona can't do that while she's driving," Blake pointed out reasonably.

"Oh. Then you hold her hand."

"The princess has spoken," Fiona chuckled, but she didn't mind when Blake's hand enveloped hers, his thumb soothingly circling on the back of her hand.

Jordan would have verbally sparred with her, told her a million crappy history facts that were unbelievable and obscure. He would've distracted her. She'd loved him for it.

Blake grounded her. Made her calm. Brought peace into her moment of stress and made her share it.

Completely different.

Absolutely wonderful.

THE PRISON HAD SEVERAL sections once they entered the sprawling barbed-wire and cement complex surrounded by oceans of manicured green grass.

"This place gives me the creeps. I'm so glad Hannah is asleep," Blake hissed. "Like if I go in, I'll never get out."

Fiona realized that would be soul-crushing to a man like him, a man constantly on the move in his own free little universe. "I can go in."

"No. No, if something happens, just take care of Hannah for me."

Nothing is going to happen. I can't lose another— Fiona wouldn't allow her brain to complete the thought. "It's very safe. And they said he's due to be released next week. We could wait."

"But if we wait, Reyes might try something desperate." Blake squared his shoulders and pushed himself out of the car.

Fiona was glad she was sitting. Her knees suddenly felt like rubber as she watched him standing there, the epitome of the man defending his family and facing his fears. "I'll be praying for you, and I'll have my phone on." She looked over her shoulder. Hannah had dozed off about fifteen minutes ago and the nap looked like it was going strong. "I'll speak softly."

"My gosh. This guy is going to wonder what the heck I'm doing here. He doesn't even know me. How did you get him to see us?"

"I told him I wanted to ask him some questions about qualifying for early parole. Technically, it's not a lie!" Fiona bit her lip. "I do want to know if there's some reason his five-year-sentence is being shortened to three."

TYLER HANES WAS A HANDSOME man, even on the screen of her phone. He wore a gray polo shirt and his reddish-blonde hair was curly and close-cropped. Fiona mentally cheered, "Bingo!" when she saw him and 50% of Hannah's looks were magically accounted for. She was a beautiful blend of Tyler and Olivia.

"I thought we'd be doing this through plexiglass," Blake said, his voice tight and high with forced cheer.

"Some prisoners, yes. I'm considered low-risk and a good role model. When I have visitors, we can sit in the recreation room at a table as long as the guards supervise us." Tyler turned to wave to someone, presumably the guard. "So, this is an interview about how to get early parole? I have to tell you, my case is unusual. I agreed to reveal the whereabouts of jewelry and cash that were taken during a robbery I was involved in. I also offered to testify about the other people who were involved. I had a meeting with the D.A. a month ago, and I'm supposed to meet with my lawyer today. Once they verify the accuracy of the information I provided, they're going to grant me early parole—guaranteed." Tyler heaved a sigh. "And that's it really."

Blake hesitated. "That's good for you. Um. That isn't all. So. We've been looking at your record and it states that you know some people who've been threatening my foster child and me."

"Whoa. Whoa, buddy, I can't help you there. I'm no kingpin! I was strictly small-time. Did a little, sold a little. Whatever this guy is doing, I can't help you with it."

"His name is Hector Reyes, and the little girl's mother was Olivia Thompson. She has bright red curly hair, beautiful blue eyes, and freckles on her nose. And Reyes says he's the father and if I don't give her to him, bad things are going to happen." Blake laid everything out in one low rush, anger seeping into his tone.

Tyler blinked and gasped, hand to chest, half-rising, then falling back into his seat. "Olivia had a baby? When? They told me she died!"

Fiona stepped in. "She did, Tyler. We're so sorry. Were you close to her?"

Tyler shook his head, then nodded. "I can't believe this. Yes, yes, we were close, but not for long. She was using here and there, getting stuff from Hector and his buddy Kenny. I was more in it for the money." Tyler rubbed his eyes suddenly. "She didn't tell me she was pregnant. She... Well, I got clean when I came here. I joined the Prison Fellowship ministry, too. The whole 'convict finds God' story, that's me. I wrote to her and sent her a lot of the literature they sent me. I told her I thought she should stop using before she ended up here, or worse. I called Reyes, too, but he just wanted to make sure I wouldn't rat him out." Tyler blushed. "I didn't, for a long time. I know no one likes a snitch, and I wanted to pay for what I'd done... but then," the young man shrugged, "I kept learning more about the Bible. I wanted to atone. Repent. Make amends. I can't do that without making sure the people I robbed get their stuff back... and I can't let Hector and Kenny keep selling drugs to people, letting more people get hooked. I don't care if people label me a 'snitch.' God is going to call me a good and faithful servant—one day."

Fiona sniffled in, moved by Tyler's story. "That's wonderful."

The wistful expression on his face hardened. "Reyes and King don't think so. They know they'll lose the car wash—that's their front. Plus, selling to college kids at all the parties. I warned them to stop. I told them I still had friends on the outside who'd let me know if they were dealing—and they did. They are."

Blake interrupted with a thump of his fist to the table. "Never give the bad guys a warning, idiot!"

"I didn't want anyone to be in a place like this! I figured maybe they'd stop if they knew the police would get involved!" Tyler protested, voice rising.

"Settle down!" A loud voice called from off-screen.

Fiona knew the guard was giving them a warning, and she made a shushing motion. "Blake, Hannah's asleep."

"Hannah. Hannah? Can I see her? Is that my—my daughter?" Tyler faltered.

Blake hesitated, then gave a single grudging nod. Fiona turned the phone to the backseat and gave the prisoner a quick view of the sleeping child.

"Look, Reyes and King are obviously still dealing and who knows what else. They must have planned to use Hannah to keep you silent."

Tyler's lips were a thin white line. "It's a good thing you kept her safe and I didn't know about her. I already talked to the DA awhile ago. They've been investigating, I'm pretty sure. But, Reyes and King were right. I wouldn't let anything happen to her."

"If you don't want anything to happen to her, then you have to establish that you're the father. Then you can take care of her, once you're out. I mean, once you jump through all the hoops the state foster care system will require you to jump through."

"And the parole people," Fiona chipped in, although she had little experience with what that might entail.

"What? I— Me? Be a father? I mean, I'm the father, but I'm not a good one! I wouldn't let anyone hurt her if I could help it, but I can't raise her! I don't have a home or a job. I don't even know if I'll be staying in the state. I thought I would get far, far away from bad influences. My grandmother was going to let me camp out on her couch in Tulsa." Tyler put his hands to his head, eyes wide, skin pale.

He was clearly overwhelmed, but Blake's reaction was the opposite. Relief washed over his features.

"Mr. Hanes. Tyler. I would be honored to raise your little girl like my own, and let you build a good relationship with her over time. I want to adopt her. My adoption hearing is this month, and Olivia didn't list your name on the birth certificate." Blake hurried past that part, seemingly unsure if it was positive or painful given the man's circumstances. "I would like to proceed with the adoption if you're willing."

Tyler nodded, then frowned. "I'm not *legally* her father?"

"Well, no, but—"

"I'd like to confirm that I'm the dad... but I'd like to wait until next month. *After* your hearing. Unless you need me to testify or something earlier? Do you need me to write a letter saying that it's okay with me? Because it is. I want to know Hannah—someday. Not yet. Maybe I can just be a good friend. An uncle-figure."

Blake reached across the table, dropping the phone with a thunk. Fiona could see a blur of figures as Blake embraced the man, his shoulders shaking. Soon a third figure joined, sternly telling them to sit back down and put their hands on the table.

"Thank you! Thank you so much. You have no idea how much it means to me that Hannah can stay with me. However long it takes or however we do it, with letters or tests, or whatever—I want to adopt her." Blake's hands scrubbed across his weary but relieved face.

"Well, that's what I want too, believe me. I'm barely getting myself together. I don't want to mess up her life on top of it. I'm glad you and your wife are there for her."

Fiona made a noise of protest, but the phone was still lying on the table. She waited for Blake to explain.

He didn't.

Chapter Thirteen

Reyes and King were arrested.

Tyler's parole hearing went well, and he contacted Blake before he left town, providing a paper drawn up by his attorney, granting his approval for the adoption, terminating his parental rights, and saying his DNA was on record with the state system.

Fiona never asked about the bit of conversation she'd overheard while Blake's phone was resting on the prison visitor area's table.

It was a natural assumption on Tyler's part. Maybe Blake didn't want to go into the painful situation and relive the death of his wife. Maybe Blake didn't want to explain their strange relationship. What was she, after all? A helper? Another victim of Reyes or King (who owned a black pick up with a sagging bumper)? A babysitter?

But curiosity was killing her, and it seemed to grow worse as the adoption hearing loomed and Mother's Day approached.

"WE'RE GOING TO GO SEE my parents next week for Mother's Day. I'm guessing you'll see yours, too?" Blake dumped kibble into a puppy "trough," and Fiona enjoyed one of her favorite sights—five stubby little Cairn terrier tails wagging in puppy joy as they scarfed down their dinner.

"I will. Jordan's mother usually meets us. It's... it's not a happy occasion these days."

"Ahem. Hrm." Blake coughed, opened his mouth, and then asked in a hoarse voice, "You thirsty?"

She wasn't, but she thought Blake was about to choke on something. Sawdust in his mouth, maybe? "Let's go get some ice water. Hannah insisted on putting mint leaves in it again."

"My favorite, water with mint and ice. I'm... I'm not exactly fancy, huh? I mean, we grow the mint here."

Fiona cocked her head. When had she ever called Blake fancy? Or wanted him to be?

"Jordan's web series was amazing. He was a world traveler and a writer. A professor who always made history fun."

Her eyebrows drew together. Why would Blake compare himself to her late husband? "He'd be so happy to hear you say that."

"Mhm." Blake chugged his ice water so fast that it dribbled out of the sides of his mouth and stained his crimson t-shirt.

"Blake, are you okay?"

"Yes! Of course. I... Uh. I was wondering if maybe all of our mothers could meet up somewhere this Mother's Day? You know, it's Hannah's first Mother's Day without a mom, and the adoption hearing is the Friday before. It'd be perfect if..." Blake chugged his water again. "Sorry. I must've gotten overheated today."

Fiona looked outside. It was almost mid-May, but the day had been cool and a bit overcast. "My mom? And Jordan's mother? You want us to come to a Sunday lunch or something on Mother's Day?"

"That's dumb, huh? Just forget about it," Blake said hastily, almost scrambling across the kitchen to put the pitcher of water back in the fridge.

"It's very sweet! It's not dumb." Fiona's heart was touched by the idea. "Seeing Hannah might cheer my mother and mother-in-law up, actually. They both want grandchildren so badly, but even getting to fuss over a little one for an afternoon would be a bright spot on an otherwise rough day."

Blake nodded, opened his mouth, and said nothing.

Fiona groaned. "Out with it. You are trying to tell me something or trying not to tell me something. Which is it?"

Blake paced.

Her stomach dropped. "Oh no! Is it the adoption? What—"

"It's fine! It's all fine. The lawyer is proceeding with the case and he's entered Tyler's letter into evidence. I haven't heard from Reyes, and you know that your description of King's truck helped nail an additional vandalism and theft charge on him."

"So, what's wrong?" Fiona was bursting to ask if Blake wanted her to get out of his life now. It had been a whirlwind month, and he no longer needed her—but now they saw one another almost every day and talked even more often than that. They had become a habit.

Sometimes you need to break habits.

But then why ask us all over for Mother's Day?

"Did I do something wrong?" Fiona pressed, blocking his pacing path.

"You did so much right! But I haven't known you very long. That doesn't matter to me, but then again, I'm a simple kind of guy. When I want something, I do something about it. I don't need much to make me happy." He cocked his head, a bemused, melancholy grin on his tanned face. "That's not you. You're all Ivy League and ancient ruins, research, and you have a beautiful piece of property, and Jordan's path is on it..." Blake reversed and was now pacing in a circle.

Fiona's mouth dried out. "I'm not fancy. I'm just useless with tools and pottery. If I had to earn a living by gardening, I'd starve."

Blake let out a single shout of laughter, then sighed. "I love the way you make me laugh. The way you make me think. I love all that stuff about you."

Through lips that were suddenly Sahara-dry, Fiona rasped, "I love the way you make me think. And how comfortable I am with you and Hannah. This was the bright spot in my life after three years of storms." She stopped speaking, throat too full, heart pressing up into it.

Blake nodded, stopping, staring at her.

In the silence, Hannah wandered in, crayons spilling out of a pink pencil box as she made her way through the kitchen. When she noticed neither adult was speaking, she stopped and looked from one to the other.

"Did you ask her?"

Fiona leaned on the wall for support. *Ask me? Ask me what?*

Blake shook his head, pop-eyed and panicked.

Hannah said no more, dropping her box with a happy little hum and going out to the porch. When she came back, she had Macbeth by the collar, pulling him along as he trotted contentedly beside her.

"Okay, we'll ask together."

Blake seemed to come alive, running forward. "Hannah, sweetie, I haven't—"

"Can you be my mom and can Daddy be Macbeth's daddy?"

"Oh! Oh, my goodness." Fiona was suddenly sitting on the floor with her dog and Hannah climbing into her lap, but she had no recollection of her knees bending or her brain telling her body to sit. "I want to, b—"

"You do?" Blake yelped, crashing next to them, taking the trio in his arms.

"Well, yes! But that's not how this works. You have to be in on the deal," Fiona half-laughed, half-whimpered, wiping at her eyes. Macbeth licked her chin.

"That's okay. Daddy wants to ask you to be the wife and he'll be the husband, and Biscuit and Macbeth get married, too." Hannah explained with the confidence of an almost three-year-old who believes she knows everything.

"Hannah!" Blake cried, clapping a hand to his forehead. "Honey, that's not how you ask!"

Hannah hung her head for a second. "Sorry. Pwease?"

Fiona hugged her tight. "That was very good manners." She looked over the top of Hannah's head. "I'll tell you my answer in just a minute, okay? I have to ask Daddy a question."

Hannah pouted, but scooted away, collecting her crayons.

"I'm so sorry, Fiona! I honestly didn't put her up to it, I promise you. But I asked her if she'd like it, because... I don't know. I thought that's what single parents have to do when they meet someone."

"It's okay. But I don't want you to ask me just because Hannah's attached. I'd stick around even if it was just as a friend." Fiona realized Blake was still sitting close to her. Very close. His arm was layered over her shoulders.

"I wanted to ask you with or without Hannah. When Tyler Hanes admitted he was probably the biological father, my heart shattered. And I thought to myself... 'I might lose Hannah. I hope I keep Fiona.' I want you. I l-love you," Blake stumbled over the word and clamped his lips shut as if dreading her response.

She didn't have one. Not one in words.

Fiona twisted her head and planted a long, sweet kiss on Blake's lips.

Hannah whooped and Macbeth barked, setting off the rest of the canine chorus. "That means you're sweethearts!"

"Yes, it does," Fiona declared, crossing her arms and daring Blake to argue.

"No argument, Fiona. So. Hrm. I'd better take my turn. Will you marry me? Not right away, but when you want to? Will you?"

"Daddy! Ask nice!" Hannah hissed, still doing a happy stomp across the kitchen floor.

Fiona giggled as Blake put his head in his hands for a brief second. "I'm sorry. Will you marry me, *please*?"

"Yes! I would love to be your wife and Hannah's mom." Fiona smiled at the jubilant child. "And Macbeth would like to be daddy to those puppies and Biscuit's sweetheart, too."

She was laughing, Hannah was squealing, and Blake was peppering her face with kisses, cupping her head in his hands.

For the first time in a very long time, Fiona felt like she wasn't spinning in circles. She was back on the road, moving forward. It was a surprising journey that she couldn't have planned. She didn't have a map or know the way.

But God did.

"We should have ice cream. We have to celebrate," Blake pulled her to her feet, beaming.

"Amen to that."

Epilogue

The judge banged his gavel with a happy smile. This was the sort of case he loved—but he had no idea how he was going to get all of these people and their dogs into one picture, and the picture was his favorite part.

"You're official, folks. Now, little lady, will you sit on my bench up here? You can hold the gavel if you're very careful." Judge Erlich hoisted Hannah onto his lap and then sat her on the wooden bench that faced the courtroom, her legs popping out of a white dress with lavender and pink roses on it. She held the gavel and beamed.

"Dad, Mom, let's have you here next to me." The judge motioned Fiona and Blake to either side of him."

And then he gave up.

FIONA LAUGHED AS HER parents, Jordan's parents, Blake's parents, and Peggy's parents, all holding an assortment of leashes and puppies, crowded in front of and behind the bench.

The court photographer shouted a few futile things, but it only made the puppies bark, which made Macbeth bark, which made Blake let out an ear-splitting whistle.

"Good enough!" the weary photographer shouted and waved his hand for silence. "Everyone say, 'Happy Gotcha Day!'"

"Happy Gotcha Day!"

Snap! Flash! Snap!

Fiona smiled so hard her cheeks hurt. "You did it, Blake. Hannah's safe."

"*We* did it." Blake leaned across the startled judge and kissed her beaming cheek.

Snap! Whirr!

"I want copies of that one, too," the judge requested with a chuckle. "All right, everyone, off the bench and into the gallery, please."

As the families hurried into the May sunshine, Blake grabbed Fiona's hand. "Hey. I'm a man of my word. I told you that you could have the pick of the litter in exchange for your troubles. But now that you're one of the family, you have all of them."

"Which is a better deal, silly." Fiona elbowed her future groom lightly as she made her way down the courthouse steps, Macbeth's leash in one hand and Hannah's hand in her other.

"Yeah, but I told you I'd give you something in exchange for your troubles, so..." Blake paused at the foot of the courthouse stairs and got down on one knee. "Fiona Milton, sleuth, sweetheart, and terrier-lover, will you wear my ring?" Blake pulled the ornately carved box he'd gifted her a few weeks ago from his pocket.

Fiona nodded as their families clapped and cheered. She bent down and slid her finger into the ring the open box revealed. She beamed at Blake, reveling in his smile and the peaceful, happy look in his eyes, a look her own face reflected. "Blake Wells, detective, craftsman, and terrier-lover, I sure will!"

THANK YOU FOR READING. If you enjoyed this book, look for news of my other *Holiday Pet Sleuth Mystery* Series releases on my website or socials linked below!

Read on for a sneak peak of *Framed by the Fireworks* and *A New Year's Cat-aclysm*, M. Culler's other *Holiday Pet Sleuth* Mysteries!

You can find all of theHoliday Pet Sleuth Mysteries HERE[1].

---

1.   https://www.amazon.com/dp/
    B0B9SFP5KW?binding=kindle_edition&ref=dbs_dp_rwt_sb_pc_tukn

FRAMED BY THE FIREWORKS

In Shay's Point, New Jersey, the Fourth of July isn't just *a* holiday—it's *the* holiday. Sadly, crime refuses to go on vacation.

Fourth of July weekend is always busy in Shay's Point, but even tireless Libby Shay has to admit that this year's festivities will break records. Aside from the usual fireworks, the bustling beach town is also hosting a historical reenactment on land and sea. Libby's sure she's out of her mind for agreeing to host a special showing at her tourist-attraction art gallery, Seafoam Frames while juggling everything else.

It turns out... she was right. When a famous painting is stolen from her gallery, suspicion falls on Libby—and the only witness who can identify the real culprit? Weighs twenty pounds, sheds like crazy, and barks.

Can Libby clear her name with some help from her trusty pup, Fox, and some unlikely help from an old family rival? Or is she doomed to be framed by the fireworks?

CHAPTER ONE

"And on this very spot, Major Bertram Shay led the Partridgeville Militia onto a trading vessel, the *Skylark*, owned by his brother, Reginald Shay. Earlier in the day, a fishing boat had reported three ships flying the flag of the British navy had attempted to engage a packet ship headed to New York. With the threat of... with the threat of—" The teenage narrator stopped, doffed his period hat, and scratched his sweaty hair.

Libby hissed the missing word from her place behind the rocks. "Impressment."

"Imprisonment?"

"Impressment, sweetie. Back then, the British fleet would capture ships and take any men old enough to fight as conscripts—forced sailors, basically."

"But they were American. They wouldn't want to fight for Britain."

Libby gave a patient sigh under her breath. "That's why it was forced, Brian."

"But why would—"

"Brian, maybe this is a discussion you can have with Mr. Partridge during your summer history class at the community college? I think we need to finish rehearsal. Your speech starts the whole reenactment. If you don't have it right, the whole thing will start off on the wrong foot."

Brian frowned at her. "Geez, no pressure, Miss Shay."

"You're the one Mr. Partridge recommended. He must think you can handle it. Oh, look. Fox thinks you can handle it, too." Libby bent down and scooped up her dog, which strongly resembled a small black fox. "Do you want to hold her while you practice? She's very soothing."

Brian bent down and took the dog from Libby's outstretched arms, tense face instantly relaxing. "Your dog is the cutest thing, Miss Shay. But would the people in 1812 even have dogs with them? I mean, on boats?"

Libby laughed and nodded, resisting the urge to go into full-blown historian mode. It was hard when her family was literally living history, the descendants of the famous Major Shay, and the namesakes of Shay's Point, formerly Partridgeville. "Maybe not just any dog, but Fox is Schipperke cross. Schipperkes are historically dogs that patrolled the wharves in Belgium. They're called 'Little Captains.' My great-great—never mind how many—great-uncle Reginald brought Fox's ancestors back with him from one of his trading runs to Belgium. I guess it was called Ghent back then. Fox is a nice touch and her great-great-great-to-the-tenth-power grandmother might have been on board that night, barking at cannons and encouraging the men. Maybe that's why we won."

"Maybe that's why your dog isn't scared of fireworks. My dogs hate the Fourth of July weekend. Well, they like the hamburgers and hot dogs they sneak off the picnic table, but they hate fireworks."

With a thoughtful nod, Libby considered the teenage actor's idea. "You know, that could be it. She's always happy as a clam—or a dog with a stolen hamburger—during the Independence Day celebrations. Okay, let's take it from the top."

Brian put his hat back on, put one leg forward in a heroic stance, and hitched Fox up under his other arm so that her four little paws balanced on his hip. "Cannon fire sounded across the restless waves of the Atlantic. Three British ships approached the quiet harbor of Partridgeville, New Jersey on July 3rd, 1812..."

Libby settled back, clipboard in hand. Her blue eyes scanned the list, which took up several pages of lined notebook paper.

Coach Brian through his opening speech. Check.
Meet with Jake and Janice to sign for painting.
Phone interview with WSHP about painting.
Hem Major Shay breeches.
Restock business cards with QR codes by the front display case.

The list went on and on. The items without check marks vastly outweighed those marked as completed.

Grimacing as she tried to smile, Libby forced herself to focus on Brian's speech, but an insistent voice in her head reminded her, *Only three thousand more things to do by Saturday morning—in about thirty-six hours from now.*

A New Year's Cat-aclysm

Davida Maxwell has one night to make sure her entire year goes right. As the new owner of the New Hope Animal Shelter, all she needs is one blockbuster gala, complete with donors with deep pockets, to turn a dilapidated building into a dream come true.

New Year's Eve could set her up for a bright future.

Or it could ruin her career and her reputation.

When the gala's biggest donation goes missing, Davida knows that she will be viewed as incompetent at best, or a thief at worst.

With midnight looming, go-getter Davida has three goals:

Distract the guests.

Keep Sparkler, the shelter's kitten mascot, out of the punch bowl.

Solve the mystery and find the missing money!

Can she do it all by New Year's Day? Or is this New Year's Eve just the start of a new disaster?

A New Year's Cat-aclysm by M. Culler is a cozy mystery with a twist of holiday romance that you're sure to love! Check out the other books in the *Holiday Pet Sleuths* series!

CHAPTER ONE

"**I** think you should have named him Houdini."

Davida laughed as she took the black and white handful from Nikki's outstretched arms. "When I got him, I didn't know that he would be able to get out of any cat carrier ever made." Davida raised the kitten above her head and looked into the adorable elfin face with its petite features and patches of black on fluffy white fur. "No prison can hold you, huh, Sparkler?"

In response, the kitten waved his tail. Sparkler's tail was long, skinny, and coal black from the rump until the very tip, where it seemed to explode in a riot of white puffy fur. When Davida had taken in the small survivor of an unwanted litter, he had been prowling around inside a big cardboard box, his tail held up over the side like a sparkler held in a child's hands.

"Maybe he needs some other kittens to play with?" Nikki suggested.

"Yeah, that would help." Davida nodded, but then shrugged. Right now, Sparkler was the only kitten resident. The end of December was not a popular time for new kittens. "If he had been born just a few weeks earlier, he would have probably been somebody's Christmas gift."

"Yeah," Nikki said with a frown, "and back here by Valentine's Day."

Sadly, it was true. Shelters always surged with returned Christmas puppies and kittens just a few months after the holiday. Little was cute, but babies grew. The bigger the animal, the faster the novelty wore off. It was no surprise that most of the dogs currently living at Davida's fledgling New Hope No-Kill Shelter were over a year old and mostly larger breeds. A handful were younger, summer puppies bought as end-of-school presents. Now that the kids were back at school, parents were stressing over another creature to care for and kids weren't living up to their promises to walk and feed Fido. Puppies from well-off families who'd chewed up Louboutins or left piddle puddles on the carpet were packed off to trainers, dog walkers, and doggy daycare, but not everyone had those resources. The unfortunate ones ended up in shelters, blamed for normal dog behaviors when neglectful humans were really the culprits.

The original New Hope No-Kill Shelter had opened in New Jersey as one of the first no-kill shelters in the country. They had started with one branch and a bunch of foster homes. Davida couldn't wait to open the first New Hope shelter in Maine—provided she actually had the space to keep it running. Right now, the old Pembroke Manor was more historical eyesore than functional.

But after Friday night, that was all going to change.

"Nikki, are you bringing a date on Friday night? If you are, did you make him RSVP and buy a ticket, or are we comping him?" Davida asked, checking her email. Another dozen RSVPs. She forgot to pause long enough for Nikki to answer. "Yes! Officially over two hundred and fifty on the guest list. Maybe one more social media push will get us to three hundred, and that'll be capacity. After we finish renovating the place, the ground floor can probably hold five hundred. Right?"

"Uh... I don't know. Maybe ask the fire marshal? Or the health inspector? Look, about Friday night—" Nikki twisted her long, beaded braids nervously.

Davida was too excited to give her only full-time paid assistant the attention she deserved. She put the last RSVPs in the spreadsheet and sighed. "Okay, we have ten thousand. If we get another ten thousand in donations— and at least two local politicians said they're bringing big money and they want pictures taken with the press. Jenny Wheatly from The Express says she's coming for a few hours, but she's going to cover some other events, too. I'm thinking we'll have a photo op spot by the French windows, and we'll tell everyone who donates more than the hundred-dollar ticket cost that their pictures will go on the Wall of Wags."

"What the heck is the Wall of Wags? *Where* is it?" Nikki demanded.

"Well, we don't have it yet, but we will. It'll be a wall in the office with all the donor pictures. Is that tacky? I don't care." Davida marched away from her laptop and stared out the window at the sprawling two-story period home across the lawn. Right now, the old detached garage (which was double the size of Davida's first apartment) was serving as the shelter's office and canine kennel.

"Well, they're the ones who wanted pictures taken," Nikki pointed out, carrying a case of canned cat food to the back partition.

"I know, and I don't begrudge them the fame for doing a good deed. If I were rich, you *know* I'd be putting all my money into this adventure."

Nikki laughed, "You're poor and you are already putting all of your money into this adventure!"

"Hey, hey, that's not *exactly* right. I wasn't poor *until* I started chasing this dream. You know how it is. People fall in love with a dream and they do crazy things to make it happen."

"Well, not too crazy, I hope." Nikki gave her a strange look.

Davida waved the look away with a shrug. "Don't worry. I'm not going to do anything reckless. I mean, there's not much more I could do. I've already sunk everything I earned at my last job into the down payment on this place. The gala has to hit at least thirty-thousand for us to get the full matching grant from the New Hope Foundation to cover the first year's operating costs. Under the contract, we are responsible for half of the vet's salary, with the other half coming from private pay patients." Davida ran over figures in her head, bottom lip indented by her upper teeth as she calculated her gamble for the hundredth time that day, the millionth time this year.

"I got it, honey. The initial grant and your savings got us off the ground, but the gala needs to make us fly." Nikki pursed her lips, her large brown eyes following Davida as she scribbled another note on her ever-growing to-do list.

"Don't worry, Davida. You'll make your money back in—"

"I'm not worried because I'll lose the money I put in." That wasn't exactly true. Davida skimmed over the yawning pit of anxiety that made the bottom drop out of her stomach whenever she thought about losing the start-up investment. "I'm worried because without a vet in attendance and the first year's funding, New Hope's records indicate most no-kill shelter models fail." Without that money to match their initial grants, the New Hope Foundation wouldn't allow their name to be on a shelter. They had hammered it home during Davida's training that when no-kill shelters fail, the dogs and cats they were saving ended up on the streets, in unsafe homes, or worse— shelters did not share the New Hope vision, "A new life and a new hope for all surrendered animals." "If we fail, we can't help anyone. The nearest shelter is in Portland, and they euthanize any unclaimed animal after thirty days. This has to work."

"It will. Stay positive. So, let's focus on what's going to go right. You've got your dress?"

Davida nodded, re-focusing, flexing her palms on her desktop in a centering gesture. "Just came last night and it fits."

"I'm sure your date will love you in it."

"Date? I'll be too busy hostessing. My only date is you." Davida looked at her right-hand woman with a smile. "I figured since both of us are single we might as well hit the gala together. We can stand around, look gorgeous, and snarf down cheese puffs when nobody's looking." Nikki bit her lip in a gesture that Davida had come to associate with guilt. "Nikki? Did you get a date? That's fine, I was only kidding about being single and snarfing. Well, about being single. I take my cheese puff sampling duties seriously." Davida's joke didn't alleviate the tension on Nikki's face. In fact, it spread to her own. "Nikki! You are absolutely coming to this event. You wouldn't leave me stranded by myself! I know I said I'd try to get a date, but I've just been so focused on the shelter that I haven't had time to meet anyone."

Nikki turned and started looking at the inventory lists. "Well, you'll have to take Sparkler. He's adorable and he's a cute mascot. I'll help you move one of those big three-tier cages over as soon as we're done."

Davida retrieved Sparkler from the top of a filing cabinet as he toppled into a half-open drawer. "You'll help me now but you're not showing up on Friday? This wasn't the plan! What's going on?"

Nikki stopped fighting her lip and tapping her short pink nails against the polished wood of the fourth-hand wooden wardrobe they used as a supply cabinet. "John Silversmith, a guy I used to date, is in town."

"So? Bring him with you! We'll let him come for free."

"He's in town, but not this one. He's about an hour away, but that's a lot closer than where he's been. We dated throughout college, but he transferred to a different branch after his college internship ended. John's been on the other side of the country for two years, which has meant he was out of my life... sort of. We stayed in touch. We haven't gotten serious about anyone else. We haven't dated anyone exclusively..."

"*He* says," Davida muttered, silently doubting every word.

"Look, he's with Whitehall and Kline Investments and he has a New Year's Eve mixer for a new branch that his company is opening in Portland. He asked me to go with him. Don't you see what this means? He wants to make this branch a success so that he can stay here and be closer. He wants to get back together!" Nikki rocked back and forth on her pink sneakers as if repressing the urge to jump up and down like a lovesick teen.

Davida put Sparkler in an empty laundry basket that was full of clean dog blankets and bedding. "Did he say all those things, Nikki?"

"No, but it's obvious," Nicki protested, pleading in her voice and eyes.

Davida said nothing. It was not obvious to her. Men were not to be trusted, and animals would always outweigh humans in her book. She felt a twinge of anger course through her as she realized that even Nicki was being decidedly "human" right now and abandoning the shelter for a shot at a guy who was probably just stringing her along.

Well, it's her life. She's young. You don't know what they had. Just don't say anything more. A smart person would keep her mouth shut, Davida thought.

I must not be that smart.

"Don't you think he's stringing you along? He has some event in the area and he knows you're around and available. You're a convenient date. You might be the 'other woman.' He could have a different woman at every branch, just like some sailors have girls in every port!"

Nikki crossed her arms. "Seriously?"

"No. Probably not. But can't you see him the next day? He won't be flying back the second the party ends, right? Don't do this, Nikki. The shelter needs you! The animals need you. You don't need a guy who suddenly pops up and wants you to make him look good but doesn't care about your plans."

"It's not like that. We've kept in touch and I know there's no one else. We still text every day. Look, this is a sign. He's my 'one.' Don't you believe in fate?"

"Nope." Davida knew she was being immature and short with her assistant. Her answer was terse.

"Okay, how about a little bit of New Year's magic?"

All of the sudden, Sparkler let out a yowl and streaked across the floor running headfirst into the wall on the trail of a tiny startled mouse.

Buy humane mouse traps. Davida scribbled another note on her list as she groaned, "No, I'm pretty sure I believe in a little New Year's catastrophe."

DAVIDA ADMITTED IT. She was sulking. She was twenty-nine and a full-grown woman (particularly full around the hips), and she knew better than to get angry at Nikki. It was just hard watching her associate and friend make the same mistakes Davida had made a few years before. After their awkward exchange, Nikki made herself scarce, leaving Davida and Sparkler alone in the office while she kept herself busy in the temporary kennel building. The kennel was partitioned off from the office but in the same former garage and workshop on the Pembroke Estate. Their small office/kennel was a red brick building up the winding drive from the main house.

"You know I don't want to get too attached to you," Davida told the pretty little kitten with its wide eyes and dandelion puff of a tail.

"Mew?" Sparkler looked at her entreatingly—and walked right off the edge of the card table that served as her desk, landing in the open tote bag by her feet.

"Well, if that isn't an omen," Davida muttered, retrieving the cat and settling it into her lap. Sparkler immediately curled into a tight ball, its poof of a tail tip between his front paws. The fluffy tuft of fur twitched and made the kitten sneeze as it dozed off.

"Hm. You're cute. Little. Unique. Freakishly adorable." Davida clicked off of her spreadsheets and opened a new window on her laptop. The New Hope Foundation had shelters all over the country, but hers was going to be the first in Maine. Each shelter owner went through rigorous requirements before being greenlighted by the foundation. Being part of the New Hope network was awesome, but each shelter had to manage their own operating costs through charitable donations, fundraising, and offering services that the community would pay for. In most cases, vets and groomers partnered with the shelter. Some offered boarding. Pembroke Manor would make the perfect shelter-slash-doggy daycare-slash-kennel.

Especially if social media worked its magic.

Davida unlocked her phone and opened her Vid-Up app, a social media video site. She aimed the camera at sleeping Sparkler and started recording. "Can you believe someone didn't want this absolutely adorable ball of fluff? Sparkler is sweet, affectionate, and the unofficial mascot for the Briarwood Branch of the New Hope Animal Shelter. Do you want to party with this silly baby boy? Check out our website to register for the New Year's Eve Gala. Dance the night away with a champagne buffet in a real 1920s estate. Put on your flapper dress, your dancing shoes, and practice your Charleston! Sparkler and I can't wait to see you at Paws and Prohibition at Pembroke!"

She hit the post button just as Sparkler stretched, yawned, and then sneezed as his own tail jabbed him in his tiny open mouth. With a startled "Mrowp!" the kitten rolled off her knees. Fortunately, Davida snagged him before he went into a free fall under the desk. "Dear Lord, cat. We're going to have to get you a crash helmet and body armor. I thought cats were supposed to be graceful."

Sparkler kneaded her leg as he settled back in her lap. The small white claws managed to prickle through her faded work jeans, a needle-like sensation making her wince. "Okay, okay. You didn't get the memo. That's okay. You have other things going for you." Davida smiled at her phone screen. The video already had a hundred hits. "You're a social media sensation, kitty."

Back to the spreadsheets.

Pembroke Manor was officially purchased, but still in need of renovations. The shelter needed equipment, both for the kennel areas and for the on-site vet's office. They needed the first year's salary for Nikki, the vet (who was supposed to start next week), and herself.

Any extra could be used to fund part-time employees and start up a volunteer program.

She was pinning way too much on this New Year's Eve gala. What if it was a flop? At a hundred bucks a head and a three-hundred-person goal for the guest list, plus the additional donations... She tapped her calculator. Yes. That ought to get them to the threshold for New Hope to pick up the matching challenge while still covering the night's expenses. It helped that many of the locals were donating their time and talents.

Especially if Sparkler lured the people in.

Lost in worried thought, Davida jumped and almost sent Sparkler toppling from her lap when the phone rang. She grabbed the portable office phone and smiled, "New Hope Animal Shelter, Briarwood Branch. How can I help you?"

"Miss Maxwell. It's Preston Pembroke."

"Oh, Mr. Pembroke. How nice to hear from you." Davida's smile faded. It was not exactly a pleasure to hear from the middle-aged man, the son of the late Flora and Frederick Pembroke, one of the richest families in bustling little Briarwood, a coastal town in the southern region of Maine.

"Yes, fine, thank you."

She blinked at the phone. Had she asked how he was? From their previous encounters, she suspected Preston Pembroke was used to the sound of his own voice and the eager replies of the Yes Men he employed at his frozen food empire. "Uh. Thank you. How can I help you?"

"I've been thinking... I know you're setting up your little animal shelter—"

"New Hope is the largest no-kill shelter network in the country, Mr. Pembroke."

He continued as if she hadn't spoken, "But it's a shame to see that beautiful old house get turned into a giant piddle pad. My mother and father didn't fully appreciate the art deco style my grandparents envisioned when they had the place built in the 1920s."

"Ah." What else could she say? Flora and Frederick Pembroke hadn't lived in Pembroke Manor in the last twenty years, preferring their retirement condo in Florida. Mildred, known as Midge, the Pembroke's youngest daughter, had lived in a small downstairs section of the home, letting the rest slowly fall into disrepair. When Davida had first seen the property listed, she had actually believed it was a vacant, wooded lot. The sprawling two-story house with a broken-down tennis court, algae-choked pond, and weathered statuary had been completely invisible from the road.

"Midge shouldn't have sold it."

Tactfulness was not one of Davida's "spiritual gifts." "However, she did sell it. You signed off on it." Midge Pembroke had appeared at the broker's office, a tiny, gray-haired woman in a faded blue housecoat and slippers. It had shocked Davida to learn that the Pembroke's youngest child was only in her forties, but had always been a bit "simple." Mr. Pembroke and an agent from an assisted living facility had joined Midge at the office. Her brother had been impatient and blunt. The stranger from the nursing home had been gentle, explaining to Midge how she would have a safe, warm place with new friends and even a pet. But Pembroke Manor was too big for her to manage, and it wasn't safe to be alone.

"Anyone could see that Midge is deficient."

Davida bit her tongue. She'd been to see Midge several times since the timid woman had left the property and moved to Briarwood Court, an assisted living facility with bungalows surrounding a common dining and recreation area. Midge was lovely and sweet. The fact that she was also very childlike was no excuse to speak of her with disrespect. "I don't think deficient is the right word. Not at all. Your sister is beyond sufficient in warmth, love, kindness, decency—"

With an irritated huff, Pembroke cut Davida off. "Look, my parents left her the house so she'd have somewhere to live. They were right in thinking she'd never get married or hold down a job. Everyone in town knows they should have left it to me. Being a newcomer, you wouldn't know that."

Her tongue was going to be permanently scarred after this conversation. Yes, in Maine she would always be a newcomer since she hadn't been born there. But she had lived in Briarwood for almost a year, and most of that year had been very pleasant. The people in town loved their animals and looked forward to seeing something done with the decrepit old estate. Although it had become an eyesore, Pembroke Manor had once been famous for its lavish parties.

"Everyone in town seems to think that your parents did a good job dividing their assets among their kids. You got the bulk of the business. Midge got the house. Your brother got all of the vacation homes, the Florida retirement property, and rental properties. I may be a newcomer, but I pay attention."

Mr. Pembroke abruptly changed his tone and let out a hearty laugh. "You sure have got one ear to the ground. Well, I guess it'll come as no surprise to you to hear that I'm the brains of the family. Took my daddy's factory and turned it into a chain of factories in both Canada and the United States. With the supply chain issues we're facing overseas, manufacturing in the Lower Forty-Eight is a smart investment. Land in Portland is hellishly expensive, but Pembroke Manor isn't too far. If I clear cut all the woods, ripped up the lawns, and bulldozed the estate, I could have a new factory within driving distance from Portland and a few hours from Boston. I'd like to buy the place back."

Davida dropped a heavy hand into her lap, startling the sleeping kitten. She spun in her chair, the motion of her body echoing her whirling mind.

But this place is perfect!

I don't want him to rip it up, even if he did live here as a kid! It's too beautiful.

Clearcut the woods? What will all the wild animals do?

Bulldoze the house? I've already got a dozen strays housed on site. I've hired a vet. I've hired Nikki. Heck, I've hired myself. This is my dream job and my dream. Period.

"I'm afraid I'm not interested."

"I'll pay you half-again Midge's selling price. The original selling price. $300,000."

"Oh."

Davida swallowed as the sound of imaginary rustling cash filled her ears. That was tempting. She'd been able to negotiate the purchase price of the property down to $180,000, so this offer was more than generous. But she'd already begun renovations, and she couldn't put a price on the blood, sweat, and tears she had invested. This property had so much potential, with space for the dogs to run, a place for the vet's office, a place to start boarding and training facilities, and more. She doubted she could find another property even half as suitable. If they kept the ballroom and kitchen intact after the big gala on New Year's Eve, they could even offer it up for events. Not many people would take advantage of it, but then again, she'd been to birthday parties at the SPCA as a kid and seen some famous people get married at zoos and museums. Why not have your special event at a beautiful animal shelter?

"Wh-what is it that you'd want to do with it again?" Davida stalled as she opened her operating costs and start-up costs spreadsheets. She scribbled figures on a pad as Pembroke lost his good-natured tones and repeated himself.

"I'm tearing down that old wreck of a place and putting up a factory, Miss Maxwell. It'll be good for the economy. Lots of jobs."

Her brow wrinkled at his last declaration. A lot of people in town had mentioned Preston Pembroke's factory, just outside of town, off of

295 North. Despite the local ties and the reasonable commute, only a few people in town worked there, claiming it didn't pay a living wage.

"I'm sure there would be plenty of jobs. But I'm not interested in selling at that price. I would need to scramble to find new premises and the approval period for a shelter to be approved by New Hope is usually around twelve months. I've already hired staff and started renovations. $400,000 would be the minimum I'd take." She crossed her fingers behind her back, as if the snarling man on the other end of the phone would be able to see her deception. In reality, she'd take less if she had to, but she *didn't* have to.

"That's hogwash. You're a greedy little—"

"I'm perfectly serious and not at all greedy. You're a businessman. I bought a property in need of massive renovations, and I've started them. To get approved for a new location with the minimum of required staff and equipment, I'd need to purchase a turn-key operation in a location zoned for animal facilities. That takes me right out of anything residential or highly industrial. Finding the perfect building in the perfect location will cost more. I'll need to recoup my outgo and pay off the contractors I've already hired. You know all this."

"But doubling your price is ridiculous. How much could you possibly spend on a bunch of animals?"

"You'd be surprised. Do we have a deal?" *Please say no.*

He said no, in a very colorful manner that forced her to hold the phone away from her ear.

"You took advantage of a senile old woman!"

"You were there! You told her to sign! Also, remember that when I showed up in that office to sign the paperwork, I'd never met you or your sister! I'd dealt with a realtor. Who got her that realtor? Who told her to accept my offer? Did you just want the money so that Briarwood Court would take her?" Davida demanded, rising and pacing with Sparkler under her arm.

Preston made a choking, snorting sound. "That's slander."

"Are you sure those weren't just *questions*? I asked if that's why you rushed through closing the deal for Pembroke Manor. Most private assisted living places expect you to pay up-front and out of pocket." Davida warmed to her topic. Sparkler, clearly enjoying a good performance when he saw one, dug his little claws in and made his way up to the collar of her worn pink overshirt, draping himself over one shoulder and headbutting her free ear.

"I... I..."

"You don't like when someone has no reason to say 'yes, sir, no, sir, how high, sir?' Do you? Well, I don't like being guilted at for wanting a fair deal. I went to see Midge a few weeks ago, and she looks like a different person. She's happy with new friends and a new dog, too." One of the shelter's first surrenders had been a senior terrier who wanted a nice human to snuggle with. Midge, apparently having been left alone in the old Pembroke Manor as it slowly rotted around her, had fallen in love the second she met the dog.

"You've been to see my sister? You gave my sister a *dog*?"

"Apparently more recently than you have. Mr. Pembroke, you have your answer. The building is not for sale."

Silence.

"You're going to regret this."

Davida hung up. "Probably." She noticed her hands were shaking. "Nikki?"

Crap. It was after five. "Come on, kitty. I need caffeine."

Do you love romance and historical mysteries, too?
Read on for a sneak peek of *The Undertaker's Daughter* by M.
Culler, published by The Wild Rose Press.

The Undertaker's Daughter

Harkness and Sons stood apart from any other building in the crowded corner of its East London dwelling place. It was as if fate had decided to protect the surrounding citizens from rubbing shoulders with death's earthly representatives.

Oh, it was all too true that death and the East End were no strangers. Her squalid yards and overflowing doss houses meant nightly contributions to the body merchants who would take the poor and unfortunate inhabitants to their final destination, not one of the overflowing and foul city churchyards, but to large baskets outside of hospitals and anatomy clinics where porters would collect them in the morning. Aspiring surgeons would spend days dissecting and breaking down a body, faces wrapped in camphor-soaked cloths to block the stench. When flesh was properly separated from bone, everything was sewn up in sturdy cotton sheets and buried in a giant pit on the far reaches of the hospital grounds.

Not so for the clients of Harkness and Sons. Reginald Harkness, Proprietor, Undertaker, and Director of Funeral Services, had a state-of-the-art facility for the dearly departed. No more calling for the undertaker, the coffin-maker, the shroud-maker, the feather-wavers, and the funeral carriage as separate entities. Harkness and Sons would supply all the services required for one fee, a one-stop shopping experience for the recently bereaved.

Unfortunately, Mr. Reginald Harkness, a distinguished man with an appropriately sympathetic face, was also a *one-man* operation. He was the only remaining son of Harkness and Sons, a reputable firm of undertakers since His Majesty George III's time. Fathers and sons had kept the business going, but now it seemed that its doors would be shuttered when Mr. Harkness joined his clientele.

No daughter of his would run the family business—even if she seemed oddly keen to do so.

"CHARLOTTE! CHARLOTTE?" Reginald poked his head into the kitchen. Clean. No smells of cooking. He sighed. "Charlotte, are you—" The brassy pealing of the bell from the back garden made Reginald abandon the search for his daughter.

Most women, certainly women with a clever mind like Charlotte's, should have been pursuing studies suitable to her sex, perhaps art, music, or sewing. The business made a good income, enough to help the girl set up her own shop. She could find employment as a seamstress or perhaps a milliner? A florist would have been ideal as he would have loved to supply flowers for the funeral carriages as well.

He had no illusions that Charlotte, even though she was radiantly beautiful to his proud paternal eyes, would easily find a husband. Who would come to pay her court here, with coffins in the small showroom that had once been his late wife's parlor and open-sided carriages coming to the back gate instead of lovesick boys with bouquets?

Speaking of carriages, Mr. Bartlesby was just coming to collect the coffin and shroud for the late Mr. Samuels. "Charlotte."

"Yes, Father?" A sweet face with wide blue eyes and curling golden hair arranged in a mass of pins atop her head poked around the door from the "laying-out" room.

Mr. Harkness jumped. "What are you doing in there?"

"Keeping Mrs. Perkins company until the vicar comes to collect her this afternoon."

"Charlotte, I've told you—"

"I know the spirit has gone on, Father, but imagine what it must've been like, to live ever so long and then to be taken ill so quickly and that mean landlady unwilling to leave her lie until the gravediggers could prepare a space in the churchyard. The cheek."

Her father rolled his eyes heavenward. "Charlotte, a lady mustn't say things like that."

An impish grin crossed her face. "At least I didn't say blo—"

"Dear me. Listen, Mr. Bartlesby is here, and I must go collect the late Mr. Samuels. The vicar won't come until after tea. If he's early, give him a cup of tea and a biscuit—"

"We're out of biscuits."

"Then be useful and bake some biscuits, finish sewing those shrouds I've been reminding you about for a week, and take some money to the flower stalls and get the usual." He swiftly kissed her cheek, jamming his black silk top hat on his head. "You forgot to steam the brim." One side of the brim had lost some of its elegant curl.

"Yes, Father, I will." Charlotte ducked her head to kiss his cheek in return, mindful not to knock the hat askew.

"Thank you. And Charlotte?"

"Yes?"

"For heaven's sake, don't let the vicar catch you 'chatting' to the dearly departed."

As her father hurried away, Charlotte sighed. "It's not my fault. It's not like I *start* the conversations. I'm simply too polite to ignore them."

CHARLOTTE ROLLED OUT shortbread biscuits. They were easy to make and her father's favorite. She was debating whether to run to the flower stalls in the market or put the leg of mutton in for supper.

"When Mr. Perkins worked for Smithfield, we had such lovely chops and all the tripe you could ask for, calves' feet, too. But cruel to the beasts, they were."

Charlotte sighed. Mrs. Perkins was a very chatty soul—literally. "Isn't he waiting for you?"

"Oh, I imagine so, dear, but you were so kind to come and settle me down when I found m'self all discombobulated, neither being here or there, you might say. A nice light hand with the dough you've got. Make someone a good wife."

"Thank you." It was no point in arguing with the gregarious and nebulous voice inside her head. She was not the marrying kind. She was the kind that was one step away from a permanent spot in an asylum, or at least the Yorkshire Dales.

The Yorkshire Dales were where her mother's sister, her aunt Kate, lived with her strapping farmer husband and their three enormous sons. To her father's way of thinking, the place radiated wholesomeness, clean air, sound bodies, and sound minds. It was the latter he believed Charlotte was lacking.

"I'm not mad, you know," Charlotte muttered.

"Are you talking to yourself? Sign of being touched in the head," Mrs. Perkins tutted.

"I'm not touched. You're here, aren't you?"

"I seem to be. S'pose it's because I haven't been properly buried. Do you think that's why?"

She slid the biscuits into the black-leaded oven and shut the door with a bang. Charlotte wished she could answer in the affirmative, but it hadn't been the case. Her mother had died years ago now, and she still heard her voice sometimes, felt her presence like a fleeting shaft of sun when passing by a window on a bright day. Her governess, whom she'd called Auntie Molly, had died four years ago and never made a peep or an appearance.

"I think that's why," Mrs. Perkins continued. "Makes sense, don't it? That must be why there's ghosts at places where wars were fought, haunting the battlefields. Some like as never got buried the proper way."

"Then why do they think the Tower is haunted? The executed were buried." Charlotte was beginning to feel cross. Most of the spirits who decided to speak to her needed a simple nudge, a little kind explanation. You've passed away. Your soul must go on. Yes, the body is in good hands, my father is the best in the business. But some... She fetched her hat and shawl with a sigh. "I'm going to go out as soon as the biscuits are baked."

"What? And waste all that good fire you've got going? Mutton ought to be roasted long and slow, dearie."

"I'll build another fire up." Impatience crept over Charlotte.

"Must be nice for them's that can."

Charlotte turned toward the direction of the nebulous presence, feeling its location rather than being able to see the owner of the scolding matronly voice. Mrs. Perkins' tone held quiet disapproval.

Charlotte told herself that was the bulk of her troubles.

I can't please anyone, alive or dead.

She was quite relieved to leave the house and hurry through the damp, chill air to the flower stalls. Mrs. Perkins hadn't realized that she could follow her and that was a bit of a relief.

"HELLO, MISS HARKNESS." Bob doffed his flat, rather stained cap.

"Hello, Miss Harkness, how's your father keeping?" His wife shuffled forward, a smile on her round, ruddy face.

"Hello, Bob. Hello, Mary. He's busy today. What have you got?"

"Mums and daisies, mainly, miss. It's the season, miss, losing the summer flowers."

"I imagine. Winter is a busy season for us, too. Consumption. So much worse in winter." Charlotte made conversation with Bob and his wife, loading her basket with flowers, buying them out, and feeling a bit guilty about it.

"You could do them fake flowers like they have on hats?" Mary suggested.

"I might have to, but they cost a lot more." Charlotte, for all the flaws her father gently assured her she possessed, was very clever with money.

"Well, you'll charge it back to the customers, won't you?"

"I suppose we'd have to. Although I was thinking we could do pine and holly. That would look nice, surely?"

"I suppose it would, miss."

Charlotte looked at the slate by the wooden cart filled with baskets and surrounded with barrels, now fairly empty. She counted out the coins quickly and passed them to Bob, who made notes in a scrawl that must've meant something to him, though it was indecipherable to her.

"And an apple for you and one for your father," Mary insisted, pressing them on top of the flowers.

"That's very kind, thank you."

"You could get a few more and make up a nice apple tart for your father," Bob hinted.

"Bob," Mary scolded. "Pushy devil."

Charlotte smiled and shook her head. "I've made his favorite shortbreads and I have to get on. The vicar will be coming after tea. I need to get the mutton in the oven."

"Ahh, pretty girl, she cooks, and she's good with figures. Mark my words, Miss Charlotte, you'll be needing your *wedding* flowers by the summer."

Charlotte laughed and waved. Bob and Mary were a devoted little couple, both with plump faces and weather-beaten hands, both missing a few teeth, and wearing the same worn brown coats no matter the weather. While Charlotte and her father lived near Tower Field, in a more prosperous area, she had gathered that Mary and Bob lived farther afield from the market, a long way down the Whitechapel High Street, right before St. Clementia's. St. Clementia's was a tiny, unadorned church that was the last bastion of respectability before squalor, opium dens, and houses of low character took over beyond the main road. The deeper you went, the worse it got. When Mary had suffered a bad fall in January, Charlotte had been all for taking them a meat pie. Her father had nearly needed to be outfitted for a coffin of his own.

A lady must never, ever, *ever* venture past St. Clementia's at night, unescorted, or at all, he had thundered, idly shredding January's *Undertaker's Gazette* in his distress.

Why he'd bothered with mentioning night or unaccompanied when he was going to add "at all" was beyond her. He didn't much care for Charlotte pointing that out, either.

"Mind your reticule and basket, Miss Charlotte." Mary always reminded her of this when she turned to leave, her voice a wary whisper, eyes roving through the crowded market. Today was no exception. "Are you heading straight home?"

"I'll be careful, Mary, and yes." Charlotte's smile was strained. Heaven only knew what girls ten years her junior were doing on London streets, selling flowers, fish, fruits, or something else, walking alone day or night, living alone, like old Mrs. Perkins. To say nothing of the boys!

But she was a "lady" of good family and respectable status, hovering around the upper bit of middle-class, she supposed. As she hurried home, keeping her eyes properly averted, she couldn't help but wonder. Was it for her protection as a person or the protection of her reputation that she mustn't venture too far from the main streets in the better parts of the city?

"Both, little bird," her mother's voice seemed to breathe against her ear.

"OHHH. OH, YOU MUSTN'T say such wicked things." Lavinia Everly giggled and fluttered dark black lashes that framed laughing brown eyes.

"But I must when you encourage me so." Her companion bent his head, his dark, curling locks combed in the latest rakish style. They tumbled forward, hiding his mischievous eyes. His lips flicked the soft skin of her ear and watched her shiver. Something in him shuddered, too. Disgust. Desire.

It was a constant struggle for supremacy.

Just like her, just like a woman. She shied away from his touch on her neck, his hand pulling her too intimately close, and yet if he should treat her with cold reserve, she was cloying and clinging, a leech upon his elbow.

Yes, women were all the same, vines choking the flowers, pretending to be so helpless when really they were the devils who would ensnare unsuspecting men. Like Lavinia did now, shuddering from his touch like a shrinking violet, but urging him with squeezes on his arm as the cab rambled over the cobbles.

A wave of fog rolled in, carrying a sepulchral stench and a metallic taste on the tongue. Outside, the driver coughed violently, startling Lavinia into speech.

"Why, where are we?" She craned her neck and drew back with a gasp. "Oh. Oh my. This is the place you wished to bring me?"

"You wouldn't be allowed in my rooms, and your mother won't have me 'round, now that she knows my prospects are bleak," he informed her bitterly. Anger flared again. *She wanted to meet but can't be seen with me in public. What did she expect me to do?*

"Why, you'll keep us fine. Mother's got money; I'm sure Father left us plenty," Lavinia said complacently.

Another dead father. His own had passed. Hardly been cold before his mother married again, a florid-faced man with a title, a baronet with a decent estate. She promptly bore him a son to pass the title on to as well. This ensured that he, the unwanted stepson, would have nothing but his late father's legacy, whatever was left that his mother hadn't spent in catching her second husband's eye.

With an angry rap, he bade the driver stop and handed Lavinia down from the carriage with a whirl of skirts and nervous giggles.

"Can't we go to *your* mother's home? Oh, no, I suppose it is too far for a night's journey. But I must be back soon. Mother doesn't know I've left, you know."

"No?" The blackness behind his eyes suddenly ticked up a notch.

"I told her I'd gone to bed with a headache. She found your last letter to me, and she and I had such a row."

"Thank heavens I didn't sign it."

"Oh, but you did." Lavinia sighed dreamily. "Not with your true name, but still. *Love*, Jack. How deliciously scandalous it is, our clandestine meetings, secretly posting letters, using an assumed name lest Mama intercept them..."

He said nothing, taking her arm and looking above the doors for a house that had a large lantern swinging from an iron hook. Any one would do.

"Is this where you stay when you come to the city?" Lavinia's voice was a tiny squeak.

"Fourpence gets you in," he said shortly, steering past leering drunkards and beggars. He pushed her roughly through the pile of refuse and filth outside the battered doorway. She let out a little squeak and all but fell into the dark hall.

A beggar's hand grabbed his pocket. Darting a glance at his floundering companion, he made a quick decision. A violent punch sent the man's head cracking into the exterior wall with a sickening crushing sound. Was it the wood or his skull?

"No matter," he muttered.

"Want a room?"

Lavinia shrieked as if someone had stabbed her with a hatpin. He rolled his eyes and dropped money into the outstretched palm of a very dirty and wizened old crone, her face barely visible over layers of lice-ridden blankets.

"All the way in the back. On the right. Out in the morn by ten or pays again!"

"Yes." He curtly nodded and steered Lavinia ahead of him.

The houses of Registered Common Lodging were usually all the same, a den for thieves and whores, or worse. They didn't care for the cleanliness if they were saved from a night in jail or a night freezing to death in the elements. The government officers who were supposed to be stamping out the filth, disease, and crime of the London slums rarely came to inspect the worst premises. If they did, they could usually be bought off for a song.

As he opened the door, he saw a stripped bed, a chamber pot that was mercifully empty, and a three-legged stool.

"Oh! Oh, we can't stay here," Lavinia hissed, her voice quaking with fear. "I saw a mouse."

"You'll see a rat in a minute." He laughed. "Come now, you wanted to be alone with me. Implored me so sweetly in your letter. How did you post that?"

"Mama has not been well. The doctor came round last week, and I sent it with Sadie, the maid."

"She didn't think it was odd?"

"Sadie can't read. She wouldn't think it odd if she could; the poor thing can barely think at all!" She laughed as if she'd said something very clever.

"Hm. But she can clean and cook and dress her lady in finery?" He kissed her gloved hand.

Lavinia hesitated, letting his lips linger as her eyes closed. He knew Lavinia was aware of his eyes on her. She lit up under his attention. She took off her hat, carefully setting it on the stool with a swish of her hips, letting her long ebony hair fall free. "What brains does one need for cooking and cleaning?" she simpered.

"Let's see *your* talents then."

"You've heard me sing and play the pianoforte."

"Very lovely it was, too. But what else have you got to offer a man?" *What else, but what you think I want, a chance to rut inside you like some filthy beast...*

Maybe you're right, Lavinia. We'll see.

"We... mustn't."

"Mustn't do what?" he led, stealing a kiss from her paling lips.

"I want to go home!" Lavinia pushed him off with a pout.

"Fine. Go home. There's the door."

"I can't—I can't go alone."

"Then stay."

"Take me home right now."

Look at her, giving orders, so haughty, her dainty nose in the air when she's not looking down at you, that is. Worst kind of woman. The blackness raged. It fell. *Let her escape. Escape yourself.*

"As you wish." He retrieved her hat and held it out to her with a flourish.

"Wait." Lavinia bit her lip, nervously twisting the ornate piece of silk and ribbon he presented to her. "I... I know you wouldn't do anything wrong. It's only that meeting in a place like this seems so sinful!"

He held his tongue for a moment, then smiled. "Deceiving your mother isn't?"

"Don't talk me round in circles, you confuse me so," she said peevishly.

"Temper, temper." He leaned as near as he had in the coach, his arm stealing around her waist.

"Ohhh." Her eyes melted as they looked up at him. One moment so innocent, the next saucy. "Kiss it better?"

His lips met hers, and the shudders took him over as he gripped her arms hard, fingers grasping hard enough to bruise.

Maybe he'd be satisfied to hurt her just a little.

"CHARLOTTE?"

"Yes? One moment, Father." She concentrated hard on her sewing. That was the trouble with white shrouds. One drop of blood and the whole thing was spoiled. She had very little patience for hand-sewing and would have preferred to use their recently acquired sewing machine if this last bit mustn't be ruched up to cover the head. Charlotte was glad that for all her father's prudence with finances, he didn't make her sew her own dresses but always gave her a generous allowance for clothing and linens. "There. That's seven done. Do you think I need to do more?"

Her father scratched his chin. "Well. I talked to the vicar yesterday after he came to collect Mrs. Perkins. The members of the parish ladies' guild are raising funds for the elderly and infirm to help them eke out the winter. Still, anyone who doesn't survive it..."

Charlotte's eyes lit up. "Oh, Father! A sort of contract?"

"I'm pleased with the idea myself. But hearing my bright-eyed, pink-cheeked daughter say such things gives me pause. Charlotte, a lady ought not to—"

Charlotte turned the topic back to business, a skill she had mastered. "A lady ought to support her father in his endeavors. After all, a father's fortunes are his daughter's favors, is that not so?"

He sighed. "Indeed, and now that Kensley Green has opened up outside the city for burials, I've made arrangements with Mr. Pottsgrove, the property manager. He'll be sending referrals our way."

In spite of her father's reservations, Charlotte watched a smile spread across his face as he discussed his plans with her. Charlotte rushed from her sewing and hugged him, patting his hand eagerly. It was the sort of thing her mother would have done when he set up to improve the place, offering more services under one roof. "Mother would be so proud of you."

His smile vanished. "Charlotte, leave the sewing for now. Another seven would be welcome, just in case. I heard rumors that the pump on Bethnal Circle has been contaminated with the fever, and you know what that means."

She nodded gravely. "If the city won't see to it soon, we'll be dealing with that as well as the consumption and cold-related deaths this winter."

He nodded in return, the gravity on his face taking a different direction. "A girl shouldn't know so much about death."

"Oh, Father. Not this *again*."

"No, I'm serious. You're twenty-four, and you're very clever. You could turn your hand to so many things. Now, I know you want to help the family business. What about if we hire a storefront in the High Street? A flower shop. Mr. Mungabee is getting older and will want to retire soon. Those two in the market you're so fond of, Rob and Maudie—"

"Bob and Mary," she corrected automatically.

"They could help you with supply. We need the flowers, after all. You'd be helping provide those two some security. They're getting on in years," he led.

Charlotte's lips thinned. Yes, indeed, her father was a brilliant man. He knew just how to make her consider it, even for a moment.

The moment passed. "I prefer to help you on the premises. There's a lot to do that you would have to hire help for if you didn't have me. I'm a good savings, Father."

"No one could deny it."

She knew *he* couldn't deny it, which is why this discussion, which had happened every few months for the last four years, never arrived at a successful conclusion.

"You'd have to buy shrouds and hire an assistant to greet the funeral carriages and coffin-makers when you're out."

Her father made a noncommittal noise. "True."

Charlotte added to the list silently. She had a calm and cheerful demeanor. She smiled comfortingly and never seemed to feel squeamish. Perhaps that was the problem. If she'd ever been truly afraid or ill around the bodies that rarely ended up staying on the premises for more than a few hours, perhaps she wouldn't be so content to stay here, and she would be receptive to her father's attempts to get her away from Harkness and Sons, away from death.

"Charlotte. You're a great help to me. But it isn't fair to you to spend all of your time here, among the dead and the funeral furnishings."

"Why?"

"What?"

"Why isn't it fair? There's a sort of grace and dignity among those who've passed. They have lived their lives, good or evil, and they're finished. Only the Almighty has to deal with them now. Nothing they can do will change—"

"Nothing they can do? They're dead. There's nothing they do. Full stop."

She flushed. Her father's eyes narrowed suspiciously. Heat rose to her face, leaving her fingers cold. She hated lying to him. Lying was a sin. But being locked away when she wasn't insane would be a sin, too, wouldn't it?

"Are you hearing things again?" he whispered.

"I hear you plainly, Father."

"That's not what I mean. You said you were keeping Mrs. Perkins company. Oh, dear Lord, Charlotte, were you 'hearing' her, not simply being your incorrigible self?"

"Lots of people carry on conversations with what's around them, Father." This was not technically a lie. "I cannot tell you how often Auntie Molly used to argue with the oven. I hear you muttering insults at your waistcoat at least once a week, but it's not at fault when you find it snug." She abruptly got up. "Speaking of snug, Mary and Bob sent us two apples. Shall I bake them with cloves or try to make a small tart, just for the two of us?"

He followed her into the kitchen. "It's not madness to mutter an odd word or two to an uncooperative button or an oven that takes too long to get hot. It's madness if you think the oven is talking back."

"I've never heard a peep out of the oven. Now, I think I'll try that tart after all. We have just a bit of lard left."

Someone rapped on the front door. Her father's shoulders sagged. Charlotte knew that her father wanted to press her further, but he was clever enough to know there was no need. Her evasiveness would be enough to tell him his suspicions were correct.

REGINALD TRUDGED TOWARD the door, heart heavy.

His poor, dutiful daughter was deluded.

Or perhaps it was some strange female malady, hysteria from spending too much time alone. It wasn't his fault that she had no siblings. If Prudence hadn't passed... "Oh, Pru. I wish you'd help her get over this," he sighed to himself as he hurried to open the door and deal with yet another unexpected client.

As he listened patiently to a suddenly bereaved widow, he realized that his business was surely the most predictable and the most uncertain of all. Death visited everyone. It was capricious about how, when, and why. It was simply too much for a woman, especially a woman like Charlotte, with her wit and waspish tongue. Throw in her penchant for hearing voices from beyond the grave? He blamed himself.

Oh, Prudence, what did I do wrong? Should I have sent her away? I couldn't have borne it.

But I must now.

CHARLOTTE BROUGHT TWO cups of tea and two biscuits to her father and his guest, a working-class woman judging by her dress and shoes. Her father was providing price options in his gentlemanly way. She knew with almost total certainty that the woman would pick the two-pound funeral. It was probably all she could afford.

"I want my Ned to have the very best. I want the mutes. Feather-wavers." She had a defiant set to her chin as if daring Mr. Harkness to argue with her. "An open-sided carriage with flowers, lots of 'em, white ones."

"Erm. Yes. That will of course run into some money. The mutes are tuppence each. The open-sided carriage is of course part of our services. White flowers, now... Hm. Charlotte?"

"Daisies and yellow mums. Would your Ned have liked that?"

The woman looked at her with grateful, red-rimmed eyes. "Bless you, miss, I think he would. He said yellow was a cheery color."

"I'll make up a nice long strand to ring both sides of the coffin. Then a nice spray on top. Understated, but very elegant. Too showy might make Ned feel a little bit of a prig, don't you think?"

Another nod, another grateful glance. "That might be so. Yes, I'm sure that's so."

"He wouldn't want you to go all out on his last expenses, not out of proportion." Charlotte smoothed her skirts and sat down beside her. "Mrs.—?"

"Bailey."

"Mrs. Bailey, Ned would worry himself sick if he knew you were spending all of your savings on the funeral. What about the rent and everything to follow?"

"I'm going to live with my married daughter in Bolton. But you've a point. There's the fares to consider and the last month paying, not to mention the doctor's bill, not that he did any good, mind you." She dabbed at her eyes with a crumpled bit of cotton edged in tattered lace.

"The two-pound funeral will be quite a nice showing and with the mutes and feather-wavers that will bring it to two pounds and sixpence," Mr. Harkness jumped in. "Have you fixed the time for the services?"

Charlotte unobtrusively shrank away, back to the kitchen where she'd start weaving the daisies and mums into long strings, white thread and green stems. She could hear her father making arrangements about picking up the body the morning of the services. Fortunately, Mr. Bartlesby, their coach driver, always helped her father carry in the coffins and carry them out if there were no strong relatives of the deceased.

He really ought to have a son. Or even a son-in-law, I suppose. Although that would mean finding a man who was both interested in undertaking and in her.

"That may be nearly impossible," she lamented to the basket of daisies on the table.

WHEN MRS. BAILEY LEFT, Mr. Harkness found Charlotte diligently weaving flowers by lamplight. "Dear, you should go to bed. You could work on that tomorrow."

"Just let me finish this last bunch, Father."

"They do look lovely. You see, you have such a talent for it! You—erm—you could do very well with a flower shop of your own. You know we're much respected in the trade. You needn't work exclusively for our family, there would be dozens in the area who would want your services. Nor would it be confined to funerals. Weddings, Charlotte. Husbands celebrating birthdays. Young men paying calls. One might even decide to stop in to catch sight of something much more lovely than the bouquets." He rested a fond hand on the mass of falling curls.

Charlotte looked up at him with a smile. "That's a fine idea, Father. I'm not sure I'd enjoy that, though. I would like to stay on here, stay with you. You know... it's not that women don't already assist, Father. Usually, a local woman has already laid out the body when you arrive. It's rarely a man."

"I don't think they're affected by it in the same manner." His genial smile turned sad. "What about studies? You can read and write better than half the lads I went to school with. You're far better in maths. There's talk of some new ladies' college in Cheltenham. You're only twenty-four. That's not too late to attend, I'm sure."

"And what would I do when I've completed my studies? They won't let a woman study medicine. They surely won't let me study embalming—though heaven knows I could do it better than half the undertakers today."

"Charlotte!"

But she warmed to the subject, abandoning her flowers and pacing the kitchen. "Would you have me enter domestic service, become a ladies' maid or a housekeeper? I've dressed myself and managed this house nicely since Auntie Molly passed. I suppose I could be a governess to some other little girls who won't get to choose a career, either!"

"Career? My darling girl, your career is written in the Bible, to be a helpmeet! A wife and mother."

"Or a judge like Deborah, or a tentmaker like Priscilla, or a seller of purple like Lydia?"

"Well... well! Sell cloth if you like. Make dresses. Whatever you wish." Mr. Harkness enthused. "Better to make dresses rather than... Erm."

"Commune with the dead?" Charlotte supplied.

"Well. Yes."

"I wish you to change the shingle over our doorpost, Father. Harkness and Daughter."

Her father's relief departed abruptly. Cold calm replaced it. "No."

"You said whatever I wish. I wish to stay with you and help you!"

"No, I said."

"Mother helped you."

"A fat lot of good she did, dying on us and turning you funny, these visions and voices and—" A look of horror bloomed on his face. "Oh. Charlotte, I am sorry. I never meant..."

"Yes, you did." The laughing eyes were hard and the normally smiling, sweet face as stiff as those he prepared for the grave. "She didn't turn me funny. She's dead, Father. The dead have no control in this world. Sometimes the soul speaks on, that's all. I'm not 'funny in the head.' You all but admitted I'm as clever as most of the men in your class at school. It's not funny for a woman to want to continue the family business she's grown up around."

She took the small lamp from the table and carried it carefully up the backstairs to the drafty upstairs rooms. Her hand cradled the tall, smoke-stained lamp chimney from the sudden gusts of air as she swished up the passage.

Mr. Harkness hurried up after her, leaving the lamps burning below. "It's not funny. No, it isn't, you're quite right. But there's no future in it."

"Almost one hundred years, Father! Don't tell me we couldn't go one hundred more. You're already far more advanced than any other undertaker in London, save maybe the ones in Kensington and Mayfair, but they have the means to—"

"There you go. Proving you could handle this business." Harkness didn't sound proud, he sounded aggrieved.

Charlotte gave her father a startled, half-hopeful look. He'd never said those words before. "I could?"

"You could. You could do it all, even the things not fit for a woman to do. I have no doubt you could embalm the most foul of corpses while chatting cheerily about what to serve at the funeral luncheon. Perhaps you'd expand our services to offer ready-made hampers for the mourners."

"Oh. That's a thought, Father."

"No! Charlotte, it's not a thought at all. It would be different if you were born a boy. But you weren't and therefore hard truths must be spoken. Let's say that you take over the business. Who will come to you? Which clients?"

"Progressive-minded ones. Women like Mrs. Bailey, possibly. They'll respect a woman's efforts." *Or would they doubt a woman's skill?*

"Who will help you nail the coffin wood together, do the fittings and the carrying? You can't drive a coach."

"I could learn those things. I could hire help."

"Which men would work for a woman? Where would your profits go?" he demanded.

"I'm certain that someone in the whole of Stepney, or even farther afield, somewhere in Whitechapel, Limehouse, or Bromley, there are two honest men who could heft a wooden box."

Mr. Harkness looked heavenward. "I was too easy on you. I let you read as much as you liked, whatever you could get your hands on, including *The Undertaker's Gazette*, including *The Modern Embalmer's Guide*. I've been a blind fool."

"Father, don't be so hard on yourself."

He turned his gaze to her. "You've answered every challenge I've set you. What happens when you wish to retire?"

Silence.

"You'll sell it to one of those honest men? You'll toss away all those generations of the family business? Because you won't have a child of your own like this, Charlotte. You won't find a husband. You won't wed. No one sees you."

"I see people all the time."

"Ah, yes. The vicars and coach drivers, the men in market stalls, the butcher, the grocer, and an occasional widower."

"I'm sorry the annual Undertakers' Ball hasn't seen fit to incorporate a coming-out party for the unfortunate daughters of the dead-mongers." Her tone was biting and bitter. *Unsuitable behavior for a woman, I'm sure, to show so much spirit.*

"Yes, there's little for you here," her father said slowly, deliberately. "The summer in London is a place of ills and infestations."

Charlotte stepped back, caught off guard by this sudden change of topic. "I suppose it is. Bodies must be buried or embalmed awfully quickly. Perhaps we could look into having the icehouse further insulated?"

"A good thought. Yes, I'll do that. I think that your Aunt Kate would love you to pay her a visit. The air is so bracing up there. It would do you good."

"I see. It will get me away from home? You?"

"Oh no! No, I want you here. Dearest, don't you know how sad and lonely I would have been? I've been selfish long enough, hiding you down here in the shadows and shrouds. You deserve a holiday. Maybe you'll love it."

Maybe I'll magically fall in love with a farmer who wants a wife to help spread manure and birth calves. "Summer is such a busy season."

"All our seasons are busy."

"Death doesn't take holidays. Will you go with me?" Charlotte turned the wick up on the lamp. Her room was small and narrow, simple. She was hardly ever in it. It was a comforting place, dark brown curtains, a red blanket, an old daguerreotype of her mother, and a sketch of Auntie Molly, and books. Books on shelves and stacks of books next to the pile of knitting on her rocking chair. Right now, there was no comfort. Her father, her dearest friend, wanted her to leave. His reasons didn't matter.

"Someone has to mind this place." He laughed weakly. "But a few months away won't matter much. We'll be together again before you know it. Unless, of course, you find you love it up there. Those boys of Kate's, they'll be such good company. Her letters are always full of their tricks, the scamps. Oh, and the Women's Institute and the Parish Ladies Auxiliary... I'm sure they have fun doing"—he groped for words— "all sorts of things!"

"I'm sure they do." Her voice was sad as she sank into the chair beside her bed. She'd never been one to faint or be overcome by the vapors, to fan herself and weakly demand smelling salts. Right now, the weight of her father's forced cheer and the sad smile was smothering her. For the first time ever, she wished her father would simply leave her alone. She wished she had a proper friend to talk to, not just him. He was so clearly against everything she had to say about this, no matter what it was.

"You might find a nice young farmer," he hinted.

"I might find a nice young undertaker here. One interested in joining the family business." The words sprang out of her mouth without thought. She'd met a wide variety of the men in her father's trade, but she hadn't found a single one engaging or attractive. They didn't speak to her like a person, more like a standard reminder of exercising their manners. A dignified and mournful sounding, "Good evening, Miss Harkness," or "Is your father in, Miss Harkness?" had been the extent of their interactions.

Mr. Harkness had been lovingly tracing the frame around his late wife's likeness. Now he lifted his head in surprise. "Yes. Yes, I suppose that could happen."

"Some of these mortuary families are quite large, aren't they?"

"Mr. Parson of Parson and Parson has six children, four of them boys. I believe a few of them are eligible."

"Well..." Charlotte stared at her tightly clasped hands as they rested in her lap. "In some cases, in some of those larger families, perhaps one of the sons would rather strike out on his own, be the head of the business, an opportunity that wouldn't afford itself to all of the sons at once."

"True. Gideon and Danvers, now Mr. Danvers has a son about your age. Peter? You've met Peter?"

"I'm sure I have." She wasn't sure at all. Her heart was pressing into her ribs far harder than her corset stays. *I don't love these men. I certainly don't love Peter Danvers, whoever he is! But I love it here. I love the work, I love my father… Many a princess marries for political unions, not for love. I suppose I shall be Queen of the Funeral Directors, forging an alliance between two noble houses. Harkness and Danvers sounds acceptable. Not as good as Harkness and Sons. Or Harkness and Daughter, for that matter.*

This is madness, not hearing the soul's echo. To marry a man you don't know if you can stand, simply to stay with the father who by every right should keep you in his home all of your days, if you don't wish to leave his side.

"Have I been a good daughter?" Charlotte asked suddenly, her voice hoarse.

Her father carefully moved her books and knitting, sitting on the footstool as his knees creaked in protest. "The very best of all daughters. Or sons. The very best." He kissed her hand, white at the knuckles, even in the dim light. "No man could ask for better. That's why I only want the very best for you. I want you to be loved and cherished. Healthy and whole. Not alone."

"You're not that old, Father," Charlotte murmured thoughtfully. "You needn't be alone. You're only forty-eight. Many a man has a son later in life. Why, King Henry VIII was only a few years younger than you. Perhaps Harkness and Sons could still—"

"Now, hush. It is unseemly that a girl should give her father such advice." He drew back, flustered. "Furthermore, in my heart and my mind, there is none who can compare to your mother. I want no other."

"A love match," Charlotte murmured, nodding.

His spine stiffened. "Yes. A love match. Ah, your mother was strong, just like you. She had your blue-eyed glare that could make a king cower." He laughed, a short morose bark. "She would give it to me now if she could hear this conversation."

Charlotte imagined she would. What would her mother say if she knew her only daughter, her dumpling, her dear little sparrow, was calmly considering making a match for the sake of saving the family business? Unlike her father, who could but wonder, Charlotte might soon find out.

"I'd like you to find a love match, Charlotte. Your mother would have wanted that as well."

"She wants me to be happy."

"Wants. Not wanted." Reginald's eyes closed briefly. "Yes."

"Being here makes me happy." Charlotte rose, helping her father rise as well, smothering a smile as his back clicked and groaned in perfect unison with his knees. "Now, the next time you see Peter Danvers, you must ask him to tea."

"Are you sure?"

"It needn't be him." Her shoulders rose and fell in resignation. "Feel free to ask someone else instead."

"Dear? This idea of happiness, it is tied to love, at least in some small part. An unhappy marriage..." He trailed off ominously.

"Now then, Father, how can you know it wouldn't be perfect bliss? I've barely met him. It's up to the gentleman to inquire after a lady's interest. He might not take to me."

Mr. Harkness clucked his tongue. "Any man with eyes would take to you, and that is partly the trouble. Any man might wish for your hand. If you take the first offer, any offer, it could end badly."

"There's no pleasing you!" Charlotte laughed and kissed his cheek. "You're going gray with worry that I'll be an old maid, meanwhile you're utterly panicked in case Peter Danvers proposes on sight. What do you want, Father?" she demanded in playful exasperation.

"What do I want? Honestly? A cold mutton sandwich."

With a sigh, she led him back to the kitchen. "I'll finish the wreath for Ned Bailey while you finish a sandwich and what's left of that apple tart."

About the Author

Bestselling author M. Culler can't stick to just one genre. She writes fantasy, mystery, and all flavors of romance. M. Culler lives in historic Chester County, Pennsylvania, where potentially haunted battlegrounds and 17th century buildings serve as never-ending inspiration. M. Culler lives for her family, her community, her students, baking, and Brit Coms. Soli Deo Gloria.

<u>Website and Newsletter</u>[1]
<u>Facebook</u>[2]
<u>Twitter</u>[3]
<u>Amazon</u>[4]
<u>Bookbub</u>[5]
<u>Instagram</u>[6]
<u>Reader's Group: Book Dragons</u>[7]
<u>Historical Heat Historical Romance Group</u>[8]

Contemporary Romance
<u>Searching Hearts II: Finding Home</u>[9]

---

1. https://ghostsintheink.wixsite.com/mculler

2. https://www.facebook.com/MCullerGhostsintheink

3. https://twitter.com/MCullerauthor

4. https://www.amazon.com/M.-Culler/e/B07MZ7KP6S%3Fref=dbs_a_mng_rwt_scns_share

5. https://www.bookbub.com/profile/m-culler

6. https://www.instagram.com/mcullerauthor/

7. https://www.facebook.com/groups/3369871793294694

8. https://www.facebook.com/groups/1704530916569869

9. http://books2read.com/u/38doWw

<u>Searching Hearts I: Search and Rescue</u>[10]
<u>The Second Santa Solution</u>[11]
<u>Seventh Floor Surprises</u>[12]
Historical Romance
<u>The Undertaker's Daughter</u>[13]
<u>Belling the Tiger(ess)</u> [14]
The Earl's Christmas Contest- Coming Soon!
Mystery
<u>A New Year's Cat-aclysm</u>[15]
<u>Pick of the Litter</u>[16]
<u>Framed by the Fireworks</u>[17]
Fantasy
<u>The Mer Parts I-VI</u>[18]
<u>The Mer Parts VII-XII</u>[19]
<u>Jack the Ripper: Demon Hunter</u>[20]
<u>Queen Slayer</u>[21]

---

10. https://books2read.com/u/mlANJM

11. https://books2read.com/u/mdd8JE

12. http://books2read.com/u/4jgvjY

13. https://books2read.com/theundertakersdaughter

14. https://books2read.com/bellingthetigeress

15. https://books2read.com/b/mZExgp

16. https://books2read.com/u/bOnKlK

17. https://books2read.com/u/mlXNGB

18. https://books2read.com/u/mgjpJx

19. https://books2read.com/u/4jPXJv

20. https://books2read.com/jacktheripperdemonhunter

21. https://www.amazon.com/kindle-vella/story/B0BZN54WL2

www.ingramcontent.com/pod-product-compliance
Lightning Source LLC
Chambersburg PA
CBHW051835130726
47987CB00002B/561

9 798215 039120